The Elder Chronicles

Volume 3

Elder Child

By

Robyn Kelly

This story is fiction. The settings are imaginary. Any resemblance of the characters or places to actual persons or places is purely coincidental.

Table of Contents

Prologue

The Elders were an ancient people. They had lived in peace for many thousands of generations on a small planet orbiting a star in a galaxy many light years from Earth. They were a well-known and respected race.

Very recently in the overall scheme of things, the Elder planet, which they referred to as Elderhome, was attacked by a fierce and powerful race. Having no defense against such an attack, the Elders were forced to flee their home world.

Approximately one thousand years ago, a small band of Elders, quite by accident, landed on the Earth. They eventually made a home for themselves in a large butte in Arizona. In the course of time, the United States Government created a reservation for a small Indian tribe in the immediate area of the Elders' home.

The Elders eventually revealed their existence to the tribal shaman and asked for his protection. Over time the shaman, and his successors, became the Elders' only contact with the outside world.

As time passed the number of Elders steadily increased until there were simply too many for the butte to support properly. To alleviate the congestion, the Elder Council allowed selected Elders to move away from the main colony and establish new colonies among the humans.

When Lisa and Nela attempted to establish such a colony in Arkansas, the result was not pretty. Lisa escaped after the last attack on her colony. She managed to travel across country with her daughter, Enela, and had, at long last, sighted the butte in the distance.

Chapter 1

A Long Night

Joe Carpenter was a long-haul truck driver. He had started driving for Trans National Trucking right out of high school and had been with them for several years. Joe liked the job. He owned the truck he was driving, a large Kenworth. It had cost almost as much as his house, but now it was his, payment free.

All of Joe's trucker buddies cautioned Joe against marrying. They said it would be impossible to be on the road for three weeks at a time and still keep a family together. Joe ignored them and married Mary, his high school sweetheart. So far, everything was working out just fine.

Joe spent three weeks on the road then had a week off at home. His home, and home base, was in Tucson, Arizona. At the moment he was on his way home after a long three weeks on the road.

Joe hadn't had any sleep for the past twelve hours and he knew he was going to have to adjust his logbook. He was coming in from Albuquerque and he had a choice. He could stay on the interstate through Flagstaff and Phoenix, or he could turn off at Holbrook and take the local roads through the reservations down to Tucson. Joe flipped a mental coin and turned off the interstate.

Joe rationalized that it was a Sunday night and the traffic would be mild. He also knew from past experience that most of this route passed through the Apache reservations. It was not highly populated and the roads were not well patrolled. If he could keep up his speed he would be home in four more hours. Joe stretched, tuned his CB radio and settled in for the drive.

Two hours later, Joe was coming into Globe. The CB had been eerily quiet, and Joe had another decision to make. He could take the road south to Tucson and drive all the way through the town, or he could cut southeast through the reservation to Winton via the reservation road. That would take him around Tucson to the interstate. Since his goal was the TNT facility off the Interstate east of Tucson, he decided on the latter course.

Arizona was full of Indian reservations. In the old days, the powers in Washington apparently saw nothing of value in Arizona and gave much of it to displaced Indian tribes. Some of the tribes were not even indigenous to the area. Such was the case with "the reservation". The original tribe had shared this area with the Hopi, but the two couldn't stand each other. The Apaches were moved in and subdivided it. To placate everyone, the tribe in question was given a separate area of its own just south of the Apache reservation.

The tribe settled the eastern portion of their assigned area, because they believed that the western portion was sacred ground and refused to go anywhere near it. In fact, in recent years the tribe had succeeded in having the western area declared a complete no-fly zone for commercial and general aviation.

A small paved road separated the eastern and western areas of the reservation. All large trucks were prohibited from using this road without a special dispensation from the tribe. The reservation sheriff was known to enforce this policy with extra zeal. Fines for a professional driver using the road could be as high as $500 and loss of his commercial driver license.

Joe knew all of this, but he was tired and wanted to get home. He decided to take a chance and use the reservation road. He had done this before and got away with it. He headed his rig onto the reservation past the sign that clearly said "no trucks!".

The reservation road was a narrow paved road, and deliberately not in the best condition. The moon was dark this night and there were no lights on the road except for those at the southern end by the turn-off to Wakulla. Joe was driving into blindness. Even his headlights did not help. Joe was just staring out into the darkness, seeing nothing. The well-tuned engine droned on quietly. Time passed quickly. The darkness, the boredom and the lack of sleep finally got to Joe. At first he just nodded a bit, then he leaned lower over the steering wheel and began to doze off.

Joe felt a small thud. It was so minor that it barely registered. He peered out into the blackness and saw nothing. Wait! There had to be something out there! Joe tried again. This time he opened his eyes. He was going off the road. The sudden shot of adrenalin brought Joe back to life. He took his foot off the accelerator and grabbed the wheel. Slowly he brought the truck to a complete stop and turned off the engine. Then he just sat there, shaking and completely exhausted.

When he had recovered, Joe grabbed a flashlight and climbed down from the cab. He could see that the left wheels off the truck were on

8

the road and the right wheels were on the sand. He walked around to the front of the cab and looked for damage.

Joe had decorated his Kenworth tractor with a row of lights around the front of the engine cover and more along the bumper. A few of those lights on the lower right side were broken. Otherwise, he could see no indication of damage. He had indeed hit something.

Joe looked around at the local desert. There were plenty of small cacti and a number of larger saguaros. He figured he had hit one of the smaller cacti. No problem. Joe always carried extra light bulbs and lenses.

Joe did not want any indication left behind that he had been here. He walked over to one of the larger bushes and broke off the biggest branch he could find. Then he went back to the road and walked back to the point at which he had first run off the road. Flashlight in one hand and branch in the other, Joe began rubbing out any trace of the tires that had run off the road.

Slowly, Joe worked his way back to the truck. He was also looking for the cactus he had hit – just to be sure. He was halfway to the truck when he saw something to his left in the desert. He aimed the flashlight at it. It looked like a blanket. Strange, but he had seen stranger. Maybe a couple of kids had come out here for a make out session and forgot their blanket.

Just to be sure, Joe walked over to the blanket and picked it up. When Joe saw what was under the blanket, he fell to his knees, stunned, and just stared at it. He suddenly realized just what it was that he had hit - a woman who had been walking by the side of the road.

It took a minute for Joe to get his act together. He reached over to the still figure and felt for a pulse. There was none. He listened and felt for a breath. There wasn't one. She was definitely dead. The body was already cooling to air temperature. Now Joe had a real problem on his hands! The death was accidental, but if he reported it, he would never drive again. He had to place his life and his family over simple legal procedure. The woman was dead – that could not be changed. He couldn't just leave her here. This area of the desert was replete with wolves, coyotes and mountain lions. If they found the body … No, he could not permit that.

Joe wrapped the body in the blanket and picked it up. It was remarkably light in weight. Burdened with flashlight and body, Joe continued his way back to the truck, brushing out any trace of his presence. When he got to the truck he grabbed a folding shovel – a treasure he had picked up at a military surplus store to clear away ice and snow. He then walked out into the desert a good fifty feet, found a large green bush and started digging.

It took Joe a good twenty minutes to dig a suitable grave and inter the body under the bush. Joe scraped the sand back over the grave and stood for a few minutes in silence. He had no idea what words one should say in such circumstances. He just quietly said, "I'm sorry!"

Joe made his way back to the truck, wiping out any trace of his presence as he went. He stowed the shovel in the tool box, climbed into the cab and drove the truck slowly back onto the pavement. Then he stopped and went back to finish his clearing project.

As Joe got back to the start of his remaining tire tracks, he took one last scan around the area just to make sure he wasn't overlooking anything. Then he saw something blowing gently in the little breeze that had sprung up. Joe walked over to it. It looked like a kind of cloth bag. He assumed it was a bundle carried by the woman. He picked it up and peered inside, almost spilling another little bundle out onto the ground.

Joe peered at the bundle in the darkness; the bundle peered back. It was obviously alive! Joe just stood there staring at it. It smiled at him. The 'bundle' was a baby, tightly wrapped, head-to-foot, in a rather dirty cloth. The cloth was wrapped so tightly that baby couldn't move a muscle, but the baby didn't seem to mind.

Now Joe really did not know what to do. He obviously couldn't leave the bundle here. He couldn't contact the authorities, even if it was just to say he found the bundle. He wasn't supposed to be on this road. Joe decided that he would take the bundle with him and just leave it at the first fire station or hospital he came to: an anonymous donation.

Of course, Joe realized, that wouldn't work, either. A big rig like his just wasn't anonymous. "Well", he thought, "his wife had always wanted a baby." A baby that they could not have. Joe got to work with the branch again and made his way to the truck. He pitched the branch as far into the opposite side of the road as he could, climbed into the cab, placed his precious bundle carefully on the seat beside him and headed home.

11

Just past the reservation was the town of Winton. Joe stopped at a convenience store there to pick up a few essentials. Now all he had to do was come up with a convincing story to tell Mary.

Chapter 2

Here Comes the Sheriff

Johnny Eagle had been the reservation sheriff for the past thirty years. His long black hair cascaded from the western hat he always wore. He had maintained a slim figure over the years by being active. He was now training his son, Billy, to take his place. Johnny Eagle's wife had died a few years ago, so he spent most of his time in Wakulla, the pseudo frontier town the tribe had built as a tourist attraction. His son, Billy, was finishing high school this year and spent as much time with is father as he could. While he was still in school, he lived at their house in the eastern end of the reservation. Johnny was trying to convince Billy that he should go to college.

It was Sunday night, the tourists had left and the town was shuttered for the night. All except the hotel, which also contained a small, but complete, casino. The casino and its bar were busy day or night, rain or shine. Johnny and Billy were making a final check of the town. They walked down one side of the only street checking the businesses, one by one. They had just passed the doctor's office. They almost ignored the shout, "Sheriff!"

Johnny turned to watch a portly Roger Wilson attempting to run toward them from the area of the sheriff's office. Johnny and Billy waited for him to catch up to them. "Hi, Roger, what's up? Something wrong at the casino?"

Roger had to stop and pant a bit before he could answer, "You've got a problem over on the reservation road. There's a semi parked over there, half on the road, half off with no lights and no warning devices. I almost ran into the damn thing!"

"What's a semi doing over there?" Billy asked. He was always on the ball. Johnny cast him a slightly disparaging look, then addressed Roger. "Any sign of the driver?"

"No, and I stopped to look," Roger panted. "If I had found him I would have reamed him a new one and saved you the trouble. I have the tag number." He handed a slip of paper to Johnny.

"Just where was this truck?" Johnny asked.

"About three miles north of the foot hills turn-off." Roger was panting a little less.

"Engine running?" Johnny asked.

"No completely shut off." Roger said.

"Thanks for the tip, Roger," Johnny placed a hand on his shoulder. "Why don't you get on to work now?"

As Roger wandered back to the casino, Billy looked at his father, "Are we going to check it out, Pop?"

"Guess we'd better," was the terse reply.

The two walked back to the sheriff's office and through the pathway between the buildings to the parking area where Johnny kept his old Korean War vintage Jeep. It was an ugly sand color, it did not have a top, the seats were well worn, but the motor and transmission were in excellent condition. It was the perfect four-wheel drive vehicle for tooling around the desert, where one could go from sand covered rock to loose shifting sand in a heartbeat.

They drove out to the highway and turned north. When they had reached a point five miles beyond the foot-hill trail Johnny pulled the Jeep over. "Where's the truck?" Billy asked. "Do you think Roger's been drinking his supper again?"

"Not necessarily," Johnny explained. "Trucks were made to be driven. I imagine that this one has just been driven off. Let's go back a ways and see what we can see."

Johnny drove slowly back toward the south. Then he pulled over to the eastern side of the road, parked and turned his blue emergency lights on. He turned to Billy, "Tell me what you see."

"Oh, damn!" Billy thought, "another test." But he climbed out of the Jeep, wandered over to the far side of the road and peered into the darkness. "This may help," his father said and tossed him a flashlight. Billy swung the flashlight around. "I don't see a semi," he mouthed.

"Use your observation skills, if you still have any." Johnny said. "What sign do you see?"

Billy felt suitable chastened. His father had stopped here for a reason. He had obviously seen something. It was now up to him to prove his mettle. Billy peered at the ground. At first he could see nothing unusual, then a pattern emerged. It was like being hit over the head with a bat. It got his attention.

Billy started pacing up and down the road, going farther and farther afield from the Jeep. Finally, he said, "It looks like a large vehicle went off the road up there. But only one set of tires; the other set must have stayed on the pavement. It probably first went off the road about fifty feet to the north and continued for quite a ways. I can't see where it went back on the pavement. Whoever was here tried to erase the tire tracks, but left behind traces of his efforts."

"Good job, Billy! I agree. Now, why did the truck stop here? And, what did the driver do?"

Billy and Johnny walked along the tire trail looking for some other signs. It didn't take long. Billy actually pointed it out, "There! Someone ventured about ten feet into the desert and came back out the same way." Johnny walked over to the spot and stared down into the sand. The actual footprints had been rubbed out, but the impression they made was still visible. "It looks like he was making slightly deeper foot prints on the way back."

The two continued along the road, noting the point at which the truck stopped. "Do you think something fell off the truck?" Billy asked.

Johnny didn't answer; he was deep in thought. Then, Johnny said, "Billy, I want you to go back to the point of that side trip the driver took. Use your light and a probe to look in the sand for anything that doesn't belong there. Go back another ten or twenty feet. I think the driver may have hit something. Whether you find anything or not come back here and wait for me. Do you understand?"

Billy knew from his father's tone that this was no test, no joking matter. His father expected him to do just as he had asked. He simply responded, "Yes, sir."

When Billy had set off, Johnny walked out into the desert, following the trail left by the truck

16

driver. It didn't take him long to find the large bush or the plot of disturbed sand. By the time Johnny returned to the road, Billy was there waiting.

"I didn't find much," Billy said. "Just these." He held out a few pieces of thin colored plastic. "They were partially buried by the driver wiping out his trail."

"Let's go," Johnny said, somewhat subdued. "I need to get back to town."

Billy was all ears, hoping for more information. But his father wasn't going to oblige him. Billy knew better than to press the issue when his father was in this kind of a mood.

When they returned to the sheriff's office, they went in through the back door and Johnny flipped on the radio. "Sheriff to Deputy 10," he sad. "Come in, Deputy 10."

There was some static. The sheriff tried again. More static, then, from the speaker, "Deputy 10."

Sheriff Johnny spoke slowly into the microphone, "There was a death in the family. You need to intervene. North end of the butte by the road. You'll see the trail. Sheriff out."

"Deputy 10 out," came back over the speaker.

Billy had heard every word and knew his father was referring to the incident they had just investigated. But a death? Whose death? Whose family? And who was 'Deputy 10'? He knew his father only had three deputies; and they all worked the eastern area of the reservation.

Billy didn't dare ask outright, but he could look quizzically at his father and wait patiently.

17

But there was no answers forthcoming. So Billy dared the ultimate offense. He asked, "What's going on?" That seemed tame enough.

Johnny looked at Billy for a minute. He sighed, as though he were weighing the pros and cons of telling Billy the World was coming to an end tomorrow. Then he put his arm around his son's shoulders and said, "Billy, if you survive high school and college and still want to know, maybe I'll tell you. Until then, you have enough on your plate. Now let's go finish that town check before we turn in."

Chapter 3

Surprise!

Thanks to the time Joe saved on the reservation road, he rolled into the Tucson facility right on schedule. Before arriving at the Trans National terminal, he had stowed the baby comfortably in the sleeper compartment. He parked his trailer at the designated dock. When it had been disconnected from his truck, all he had left to do was turn in his logbook. Then he was on his way home.

Joe had not quite figured out how to break the news about the new member of the family to his wife, Mary. He would just have to play it by ear.

Joe and Mary lived in a modern one-story adobe-style house in a small subdivision in southeastern Tucson. They had a corner lot with sidewalks out front and a large yard. There was a two-car garage that housed Mary's car and Joe's workshop.

Joe pulled the truck into the side yard and gathered his packages. What to do with the baby? He couldn't safely manage the sacks and the baby. Finally, he just shoved the tightly wrapped baby into one of the sacks and headed into the house through the back door.

"Hi, Darlin'," Joe said as he entered the kitchen, placing the bags on the counter by the sink. Mary greeted him with a welcome hug and a long kiss. Mary was wearing her favorite gingham dress. The aroma of his favorite meal, sausage and penne with garlic bread, wafted through the kitchen.

When they finally separated, Mary gazed at the grocery bags Joe had carried in. "Don't I keep the house well stocked?" she chided as she moved toward the counter.

Joe beat her to it, blocking her access. "I just brought a few things I thought we might need," he explained haltingly. But Mary could see one of Joe's purchases sticking up out of a bag. "What do we need diapers for?"

"Well," Joe began, reaching into the other sack, "I brought home a little surprise."

Joe carefully lifted the small bundle from the sack and exposed the content. Mary just gazed in disbelief as the small white face peered back at her. At last she asked, "What is it?"

"It's a baby," Joe explained, as though the answer was obvious.

"But what are you doing with it? Why? How?" Mary's mind was reeling.

Suddenly, Joe had an inspiration, "It's a gift from God," he said. "You said you always wanted a baby, and we can't seem to get the job done by ourselves. Looks like Providence just stepped in and helped things along."

"Joe Carpenter, you just explain yourself, and right now!" Mary was absolutely indignant, and just a little bit afraid.

"Well, it's like this…" Joe said. He explained that he had come home via the reservation road. Yes, it was illegal, but he had made it safely. On the way through the reservation he had spotted this bundle lying on the side of the road. He stopped to investigate and found this little baby. The child was all alone; there was no one else around. He had called out to be sure. He just couldn't leave the baby lying there, what with all the wolves and coyotes and lions prowling that area. So, he had brought it home with him. Joe always told the truth, but sometimes he didn't tell all of the truth.

Mary was still worried, "Joe, we can't just keep a strange baby. We've got to report it to someone."

"If we tell anyone where I found it", Joe reminded Mary, "I'll be fined for driving on the reservation road and loose my CDL".

"Well, we can drop it off at a hospital or fire department," Mary didn't like the idea of keeping the baby at all.

Joe had kept his secret weapon well hidden. He now handed the baby to Mary to hold. "Just look at the tiny thing," he said. "How can we hand her over to some sterile care facility? She needs to be raised by a family that cares about her."

Mary was bending under the steady gaze of the little person she was holding, but she hadn't broken, yet. "Joe, we just can't keep her. What about her real parents?"

Joe was ready, "We can just take care of her until her real parents show up. Surely, they'll advertise her loss. Maybe they stopped for a minute out there in the desert, put her on top of the car or something and then just drove off without her in the car. Sooner or later they will realize she is missing and put out flyers. Then we can give her back to her proper home."

"What 'proper home'?" Mary said sternly, "If they drove off without her, maybe they don't deserve her. Besides, if they lost her on the reservation, why would they ever advertise down here in Tucson?"

"That's it," Joe said, ignoring Mary's obvious objection. "We'll just keep her until her parents come forward."

"Well, I suppose so," Mary agreed, cuddling the little baby even closer. "But how do you know it's a little girl?"

"I thought maybe she needed a diaper change," Joe admitted sheepishly, displaying the open bag of disposable diapers. "Now can we sit down to eat? I'm famished!"

Mary pulled an old dishpan out from under the sink, set it on a chair and placed the baby in it. Then she brought the skillet from the stove and dished out the pasta. As they were eating, Mary brought up a good question. "What are we going to call the baby? 'The Baby' won't work. 'She', alone, will get old in a hurry. We really ought to have a name for the baby. Did you happen to see anything with her name on it?"

"No." Joe answered between mouthfuls. "What you see is what I found. No name, no food, no nothing, but the wrap." Short pause for another mouthful. "What do you think?" Joe countered. "We may not have her for long."

"Well," Mary considered the issue, "she will be long gone before she knows what a name is. Let's call her, Jesse, that was my mother's name."

"Jesse, it is," Joe agreed, as he said a small prayer that things had gone as well as they had, and directed his attention to the food before him.

After the meal, Joe retired to the bedroom and was asleep as soon as his head hit the pillow. Mary disposed of the leftover food, loaded the dishwasher and turned her attention to Jesse. The swaddling wrap around Jesse fascinated Mary. It was unique. It was also filthy! Joe had obviously solved the problem of unwrapping and rewrapping, so Mary decided she would give it a try. She discovered that it wasn't really difficult once you figured out all the twists and turns.

"Well, Jesse, how about a nice bath?" Mary cajoled as she put some warm water and a couple of drops of anti-bacterial soap into the old dishpan. Mary didn't have the benefit of darkness. The kitchen was brightly lit. When the wrapping came off, she could clearly see Jesse's brilliant white skin and complete lack of hair. In spite herself, Mary stared openly. By the time she had finished the bath and had diapered Jesse and wrapped her in a soft towel, Mary was almost in a state of shock.

Still, Jesse had to eat. Joe had purchased some infant formula and baby bottles. Mary mixed the formula according to label directions, warmed it in a bottle and sat down to offer it to Jesse. Jesse eagerly accepted the nipple, took a swig and immediately spit it all out onto the towel Mary was using as a bib.

Mary checked the instructions. Yes, she had mixed it correctly. It was baby formula. It even smelled like baby formula, Mary thought. Mary got another bottle and put plain water in it. She tentatively offered this to Jesse. Jesse instantly downed a quarter of the bottle. Water – yes; formula – no. So far so good, but water had no nutrient value. Jesse had to have food as well as water.

Mary tried adding a little sugar to the water. Jesse drank a couple of sips and then refused the bottle. At least she didn't just spit it out. But empty calories aren't nourishing. Mary felt she was fighting a losing battle, but she wasn't defeated. What about the formula wasn't palatable – besides the odor? She scrutinized the label. Besides the extra vitamins and minerals, there just two basic things in the formula.

Mary went to the refrigerator and pulled out a jug of milk. She warmed a little milk in another bottle and offered it to Jesse. The little baby instantly downed a quarter of the bottle. So, Mary thought, pitch the formula and concentrate on milk. She would visit the store tomorrow to see just what was available.

Mary carried Jesse back to the bedroom, cleared a spot in her lingerie drawer and laid her down for a good night's rest. Mary undressed and slipped into the beside Joe. She, too, drifted off immediately. But Mary had some very troubling dreams.

Chapter 4

Doc Baxter Explains

When Mary awoke in the morning, Joe was still soundly asleep. So she got up, showered, dressed and then turned her attention to Jesse. A diaper change revealed a little dampness, but no major discharge. Mary wondered if that could be attributed to a dehydrated state. She took Jesse to the kitchen and prepared a bottle of milk for her. Jesse drained the small bottle. Mary added some water to the empty bottle and Jesse even drank some of that. Then Mary set Jesse down and fixed herself an egg and some toast. As she was eating, Mary had an idea. She dipped her finger in the egg yolk and offered it to Jesse. The little girl eagerly sucked the egg off of her finger.

Mary drew up a grocery list and left a note for Joe. He usually slept late on his first day home, then started in on the chores Mary had left for him in his 'Job Jar'.

Mary Went to her sewing supplies and selected a piece of sheet that was about the same size as the dirty swaddling cloth. A few snips with her sewing scissors and she had a new, and clean, swaddling cloth.

Mary wrapped Jesse in the new swaddling cloth. Then she looked at the remaining cloth that Joe had brought home with her. It took a few moments, but Mary finally discovered what the cloth was for. It was a sling in which she could carry Jesse. But it was so short, and so dirty, that, Mary decided to just put it in the wash for the time being. She would just take Jesse with her in the swaddling cloth. Not quite proper, but it would have to do until Mary could get a carrier.

That was in fact Mary's first chore. She found a small stroller that had a removable carrier built in at a local thrift shop. Mary put Jesse in the carrier and stowed the stroller in the trunk of her car. Then it was off to the doctor's office.

Mary had thought long and hard about her next step. It could prove to dangerous, even devastating. Mary sat in her car in the thrift store's parking lot for some time, still weighing her options. She wasn't going to be able to live with herself unless she did it – unfortunately, she might not be able to live with Joe if he learned what she was up to. At last Mary decided it was a step she had to take. She started the car and drove to her next stop.

Old Doc Baxter was a Tucson legend. He had arrived there early in the century, fresh out of medical school. He had been practicing there ever since. He did everything from bringing babies into the world to patching up their Little League injuries to treating the cancer that put them in their graves. In fact, he had delivered Mary and treated her through most of her life. Five years ago he had retired and now lived a quiet life with his wife of fifty years. His wife had also served as his office nurse.

Doc Baxter had always worked out of an old two-story house in western Tucson, near the university. Mary drove over to the doctor's house and parked on the street in front of it. Then she unloaded Jesse and headed up to the front door.

The doctor's house was built of wood, painted sparkling white and surrounded by trees.

It had a small, but pleasant front porch where many of his patients had waited their turn in rocking chairs. The doctor's original shingle still swung on its hanger over the top of the steps. Mary went boldly to the door and rang the bell.

Doc Baxter's wife, Hilda, answered the door. She was wearing slacks and a colorful top. Her gray hair was wound into a bun. "Yes, can I help you?" she asked.

"I need to see the doctor." Mary began.

"The doctor does not see patients anymore," Hilda brusquely proclaimed, "He is retired."

"I know that," Mary pleaded, "but I really need to see him. It's an emergency!"

"Then go to the ER at the hospital," Hilda suggested. "I told you, the doctor no longer sees any patients!" Hilda insisted and tried to shut the door.

Mary was determined to have her way. She blocked the door with her left foot and all her weight and cried out, "Please, I really have to see the doctor!"

The struggle at the door had attracted the attention of Doc Baxter, who now joined the fray. "What's going on out there?" he called out from inside the house.

This inspired Hilda to make an extra effort to get Mary out of the doorway. Mary was still resisting when the doctor shuffled up to the door and joined them.

"What is it, Hilda?" he asked quietly.

Before his wife could answer, Mary did her best to work around her. "Doctor Baxter," she exclaimed, "I have a problem that only you can help me with. Please let me explain it to you."

"Please, Doctor, go on back inside and let me get rid of her." Hilda was still on the defensive. She was in no mood to be defeated by this impudent intruder.

"Now, now, Hilda," Doc Baxter said in a very conciliatory manner, "before we throw this nice young woman out on her ear, maybe we should let her have a chance to talk." Doctor Baxter sounded quite serious, but there was still a cagey gleam in his eyes. "So, young lady, just what is so serious and urgent that you have to speak with me?"

Mary took full advantage of her opportunity. "Doctor Baxter, you brought me into this world and you treated me throughout my childhood. I know that you are retired now, and justly so... but I have a unique problem that only you and your experience can help me with. I just can't go to an uncaring emergency room ... And it may be a matter of life and death ..." Mary's voice trailed off, she sounded so pitiful and desperate that she even frightened herself.

"Well, well," said the doctor, "I do believe you are John Williams' little girl, Mary. Am I right?"

"Yes, Doctor. Mary answered, more calmly. "I'm married to Joe Carpenter now."

"So tell me," Doc Baxter asked, "what is this urgent problem?"

"Doctor!, Please," Hilda persisted, "you are not supposed to be working. You are supposed to take life easy!" Hilda's German heritage was shining through. She was concerned about her aging husband and still determined to have her way.

"Could we go inside?" Mary asked humbly. "It's rather private."

"Of course," the doctor answered. "My examining room is still set up. Please come in. Apparently you are next."

Hilda just sputtered, but she dutifully stood back and made room for Mary and Jesse to enter the house. Doc Baxter led the way past the living room to an old first-floor bedroom that had been converted to an examining room when the doctor first moved into the house. The room contained several cabinets around the walls, a sink, a couple of chairs, a stool and a typical examining table in the middle of the room.

When Mary was properly seated, the doctor closed the door and put on an ancient white lab coat that had been hanging on a hook inside the door. Then he pulled on the paper that was covering the examining table until a fresh sheet covered the table. At last he turned his attention to Mary.

"So, have a seat on the table and tell me what the problem is," the doctor said.

"I'm not the patient, Doctor," Mary explained. "It's the baby. I would like you to examine the baby thoroughly and tell me what you find." Mary put Jesse on the examining table and stood back.

"But what is the matter?" the doctor asked. "What am I looking for?"

Despite her success so far, Mary was frightened, and her voice betrayed her. "I don't want to prejudice your findings, Doctor. I'm hoping that all of your experience will provide some answers."

"Answers?" the doctor mused, "Well, let's see ..." With that he unwrapped Jesse and started his examination. He listened to her heart with his stethoscope. Felt for her pulse. Listened to her breathing. Felt her limbs. Used an otoscope to look into her ears and nose. Weighed and measured her. He wasn't equipped to take the blood pressure of a baby this small, but did not see that as a special problem.

When it appeared that the doctor had completed his examination, Mary dropped her bombshell. "Don't forget her genitals."

Doctor Baxter looked up at this exhortation. He entertained the thought that the baby was intersex. That would explain the 'problem'. But he proceeded to remove Jesse's diaper and continue the examination. As soon as the diaper was removed, it was obvious the she had no navel. At this point the doctor paused notably. Then he took up his stethoscope and started listening to Jesse's chest and belly again. When he hung the stethoscope around his neck, Mary chimed in again. "What about her hands and feet?"

The doctor looked at Mary with a truly puzzled expression, but he did what she suggested. When he satisfied himself as to the status of his little patient, Doctor Baxter wrapped little Jesse back up in her swaddling cloth and handed her to Mary. Then he sat down in the chair opposite Mary and just looked at her. Mary placed Jesse in the carrier on the floor by her chair. Then she waited for the doctor.

"You were obviously aware of her condition before you brought her to me," the Doc Baxter started. Mary nodded. "Where did she come from? How did you come by her?" Mary told the doctor what Joe had said last night.

"You have a truly remarkable baby," Doc Baxter was curious, but far too old and tired to be able to pursue that curiosity. "As far as I can tell, she is healthy. But I have never seen another child like her. I have nothing to compare her to."

Mary felt the doctor was ready for the question that had been burning in her since the previous evening. "Is she human?" she asked quietly.

Doc Baxter did not answer immediately. He thought seriously about the question. Eventually, he said, "I have never seen another human being like her. But, then, I have not examined every human being." He knew he was hedging.

"Doctor!" Mary was almost angry.

"Alright, I know what you are thinking, maybe fearing, but I just can't bring myself to say it. I can't believe that it has happened. It's just too mind boggling."

Mary stood up and picked up the carrier. "Thank you, Doc Baxter," she said resignedly. "I believe you have answered my question. I trust that this will remain a private doctor-patient situation. Just between the two of us ..."

"Of course it will," Doc Baxter reassured her. "Besides, who would believe me? Even Hilda would think I was completely nuts if I mentioned it to her." He paused for a second, then asked, "What are you going to do?"

31

Mary looked him square in the eyes, "I'm going home and I'm going to take care of my new daughter. At least until someone in a flying saucer drops down in my backyard and demands their child back."

Doc Baxter just looked at Mary quietly and nodded.

Mary left the doctor's house and drove to the grocery store.

Mary surveyed the milk and dairy department. She bought some whole milk, some yogurt, some cottage cheese and a quart of low-fat for her own use. She also picked up a dozen eggs and a few other items. Once they were stowed in her trunk, she was still mulling over a decision she had to make.

Mary finally resigned herself to her fate and drove home. She had groceries to unload and it was time to feed Jesse.

Chapter 5

Choices

When Mary got home with Jesse, Joe was hard at work under the kitchen sink repairing the garbage disposal unit.

"Hi, Honey," Mary greeted him, "how's it going?"

"Umm!" Joe grunted.

Mary stepped around his outstretched legs as she put away the groceries and fixed Jesse a bottle of milk. Once she and Jesse were seated at the kitchen table Mary asked, "Have time for a break?".

Joe grunted and uncoiled himself from the under-sink area. "Sure. I think it's working now." He stood up, turned on the water and flipped the disposal switch. The unit coughed and whirred into action. Joe turned it off, got a beer from the refrigerator and sat down at the table.

"What's up?" he asked.

"I went to see Doc Baxter today." That simple statement took all of Mary's courage.

"Wait a minute," Joe said quizzically, "I know I don't spend much time around here, but didn't he retire a few years ago? I thought I saw it written up in the papers at the time."

"Yes, he did," Mary replied. "I had to really fight to get to see him today. But he is the most knowledgeable person I know of the people of this area. He delivered most of them."

"So, are you sick?" Joe was sounding concerned.

"No. I asked him to examine Jesse." Mary's voice was quivering just a bit.

"There's something wrong with Jesse?" Joe was more than just concerned. He suspected from Mary's attitude that something was going on.

"That's what I wanted to find out," Mary replied as calmly as she could.

"And?" Joe added a little impatience to his voice.

Mary hesitated. She still hadn't figured out just how to explain, but she had started this and she knew she had to finish it. She sighed and began, "You've seen Jesse. Haven't you noticed anything unusual?"

"Well, she didn't seem to have a navel or an ass-hole. At least I didn't see any. But I haven't dealt with that many babies. I thought maybe it hadn't developed, yet." Joe was fidgeting. He knew how lame that sounded.

"Joe!" Mary responded, happy for the opportunity Joe had given her. "Even you aren't that dense! Anyway, I wanted Doc Baxter to have a good look at Jesse and give me his opinion."

"What did he say?" Joe had his own suspicions and was almost afraid to hear the answer.

"He didn't come out and say it plainly," Mary blurted it out all at once, not pausing for a breath, "but he hinted that maybe Jesse's real parents just might show up some day in a flying saucer. Joe, he didn't think the Jesse was human!" Mary was almost in tears. "What are we going to do?"

Joe didn't have a quick answer. He took a swig of beer as he pondered the question and Mary just looked at him helplessly. Jesse had finished the bottle of milk and Mary retrieved it and set it on the table.

Finally, Joe said, "It looks like we still have the same three choices. I don't think this changes that. We can keep her and raise her as our daughter; we can return her to where I found her and leave her on the side of the road; or we can turn her over to the authorities."

"But, Joe," Mary said with true alarm in her voice, "if we turn her over to the authorities, they will find out what she is and she will just become some sort of a lab rat!"

"Now, Mary, " Joe said, trying to keep the conversation more clinical than emotional, "you've been watching too many of those sci-fi movies. I doubt it would be that bad."

"It would be bad enough," Mary pleaded. "I suppose if we left her on the side of the road, she would just lie there until her parents showed up."

Joe grimaced, but he had no comment.

"The only way we can be sure she's properly taken care of," Mary said at last, "is to keep her with us. Unless you can come up with something better that we haven't considered."

Joe shook his head. He was the only one who knew that at least one of Jesse's parents would not be showing up. He hesitated to think how mad the other one would be if it showed up on their doorstep. That in itself was a good argument for doing something with her, but what.

35

Mary and Joe continued sitting at the table for a few more minutes, each deep in thought. Finally, Mary gave voice to another problem.

"If we keep Jesse, we are going to have to make some preparations. She will need her own room and playthings."

"We have plenty of time to consider these things," Joe argued. "She is still just a tiny baby,"

"Not so much time as you may think," Mary cautioned. "We don't know how old she is, or how fast she will grow. Hell, we don't know anything about her. We don't even know if she *is* a 'she'."

"You may have something," Joe conceded. "So what do *you* think we ought to do?"

"Why don't you find us a crib," Mary suggested, "and a changing table, and playpen. I'll make a space in the back bedroom. We can make that Jesse's room."

"Okay, I'll borrow Rick's pick-up tomorrow and see what I can find."

Mary had another thought, "She will have to be educated," she said. "Do we dare send her to school?"

"She doesn't look like us," Joe stated the obvious. "Children have a keen perception for differences. School is probably out of the question. But that is years away. We still need to deal with today."

"But, what do we do when she grows up?" Mary was feeling quite overwhelmed by the situation. "She'll never have a boy-friend or be able to marry and raise a family."

That last comment was too much for Joe. He had a sudden thought that he didn't dare give voice to. He knew that Jesse had a parent – or at the very least a care-giver. They hadn't been wearing some alien fabric, but human created cloth: old, dirty human-created cloth. Could there be others somewhere? If so, how could he find them and return Jesse to her own kind. On the other hand, what might they do to him if he did indeed find them? "Maybe," he thought, "it would be better to just leave well-enough alone."

"Joe?" Mary was looking at him curiously. "Where are you?"

"Oh, sorry, Joe stammered, "I was just thinking about lunch. Maybe I'll see about getting those items after lunch. I'll do the flower beds tomorrow."

And so it was that Baby Jesse, by default, became a member of the Carpenter family.

While Joe was off looking for baby furniture, Mary laid Jesse down in the center of their bed for a nap. She then spent the afternoon making space for the new furniture in the back bedroom. It was a pleasant room in the back corner of the house with light beige walls and windows on two walls. Marry surveyed the room and decided that the chest could stay and maybe the nightstand. But the double bed would have to go

Mary stripped the bedding and set it out to be washed. She laid plastic sheeting on the floor and wrapped first the mattress, then the box spring. They were going to the garage. The bed was shortly in pieces and following the other items. She moved the light green area rug to the center of the room and gave the room a good cleaning.

She cleaned out a couple of the drawers in the chest and found another storage space for the items they had contained. She moved the diapers from the kitchen to the bedroom and packed up the formula to go to the local food bank.

Satisfied with her efforts, she put the bedding in the washer, retrieved Jesse and sat down with a cup of tea to watch her favorite soaps and plan supper.

Joe returned about an hour later with his purchases. He dropped them off in the garage and left to return the pick-up to his friend, and fellow Trans National Trucking driver.

As soon as Joe had departed with the pick-up, Mary closed the garage door. In her mind it would be better to deal with nosy neighbors later – after she had come up with a good explanation for their new family addition.

She took a quick look at the crib and left that for Joe to struggle with. She moved the white changing table to the bedroom and then considered the playpen. She thought of it as a place where she could safely leave Jesse while she was occupied elsewhere in the house. The bedroom just didn't seem to be the right place. It was in the back of the house and partially isolated from the normal routine. Then she had a brilliant idea: in the living room, directly in front of the television set.

The TV set was a little 19-inch model sitting on a small table on one side of the living room. If she moved a couple of chairs slightly, she could still leave the lamp table between them and put the crib in the hole between the chairs and the couch. She tried out the new configuration. There was still enough space to get around in the room, and it would be a perfect place when Jesse became interested in *Sesame Street*. If she ever became interested in television at all! Mary realized that she had absolutely no idea what Jesse would be like as she grew up. "What if she turned out to be a cannibal?" Mary thought briefly. "No – that was silly! Wasn't it?"

It was a struggle, but Mary got the floor of the crib into place and brought in the sides, one at a time. In short order the crib was set up, but not in working order. She couldn't figure out how to connect everything properly.

Joe to the rescue! He returned just in time to complete the playpen and assemble the crib before supper.

After supper was family time – at long last. Mary introduced Jesse to the playpen while she and Joe took over the couch for a little cuddling, and whatever might follow. Later, Jesse got to try out her new crib while Joe and Mary retired to their bed.

Mary was a little worried about Jesse. She had no idea whether a sleeper and a blanket would be appropriate or not. And she discovered that she had no way to tell. No matter what she tried, Jesse just took it all in stride. In fact, she did not protest anything and she didn't make a sound. Mary finally settled for a blanket, bur no sleeper. She reasoned that Jesse was strong enough to throw off the blanket if it was unneeded.

Mary was also deeply worried about any illness that Jesse might contract. If the little baby got sick, there was no one to whom she could take her. Even Doc Baxter would be no help. So the first few days passed with question after question and test after test. By the end of the week there had been no catastrophe. Jesse was still healthy – and growing, and the house was settling into a routine.

Unfortunately, it was also time for Joe to go back on the road again. As he bid his farewell early on Monday morning, Mary assured him that all would be well. He assured Mary that he would call her whenever he had a chance. Though what if anything he could do from New York or Florida was never quite spelled out. He would return, as usual, in three weeks.

With Joe back on the road, Mary soon discovered just how much little Jesse was going to change her life. Monday and Tuesday had always been reserved for Mary's party bridge group. So, after a few more hours of sleep, Mary arose, showered, dressed in a good skirt and blouse and fixed breakfast as she usually did Monday morning. Then it dawned on her that she couldn't just walk out and leave Jesse alone. Neither could she risk taking Jesse with her. Everyone would want to see the new little baby and hear all about her. She would be the star of the day.

That is when it finally sank in: what to do with Jesse when she wanted to leave the house – for anything. A sitter was out of the question. There were several teenagers in the neighborhood who were excellent with children. But they were in school during the day. And, there was no teenager she could trust to keep Jesse's secret. If one teenager found out about her, the whole county would know in short order. An older woman would present the same problem. Her parents lived in Georgia and Joe's in Michigan:

no help there. Besides, she really had no desire to explain to them how she acquired a live-in baby without the benefit of a pregnancy.

Mary went back to the possibility of taking Jesse with her. The sling was sufficient for short trips to the store. Jesse fit down into it and was not usually visible. But, her friends would insist on seeing her. How could she explain a perfectly bald, white-skinned little baby with black eyes? Maybe, Mary thought, she could claim that they adopted an albino baby from some uninhabited area of central China. That would explain Jesse's appearance. But that would also make her even more interesting, and the story would have to be explicit and ... The more Mary thought about it, the more impossible it became.

Mary changed into her usual cotton housedress and resigned herself to being a stay-at-home mom. When Joe returned, she would have one heck of a week on the town! She put Jesse in her playpen and turned on the television set to *Sesame Street*. Mary sat down to figure out what she could do for simple entertainment. Actually, she discovered, there was quite a bit. She could go to the Tucson Mall and window shop, especially when her closer friends were occupied elsewhere. She could go to the movies, to the library, to a restaurant. She could go to Phoenix, or take classes at the University of Arizona. Jesse could remain out of sight in her sling. Life would be different, but it would be good. Mary started making a schedule.

Chapter 6

Baby Jesse Grows

Baby Jesse's typical day began with a dry diaper, followed by a breakfast of a small bottle of milk. Mary would just sit and hold her while Jesse ate. Mary would eat her own breakfast at the same time. Mary enjoyed a variety of items, such as bacon and eggs, pancakes, biscuits and waffles. When Mary had eggs, she would let Jesse suck some of the yolk off her finger. After breakfast Jesse would go into her playpen and watch television while Mary tended to routine household chores.

As Mary moved around the house, she constantly watched Jesse for any sign of movement, but Jesse always just lay where Mary put her without any significant motion. Mary did not know what to expect. She would gladly have given her eyeteeth just to hear Jesse cry – once. But Jesse remained silent.

Every so often Mary would offer Jesse a bottle of water. Sometimes Jesse would take it, sometimes not. There was never any pattern.

For lunch Jesse had cottage cheese or yogurt and a bottle of water. Mary would have a salad or sandwich. Jesse never showed the slightest interest in anything Mary ate.

After lunch they would both watch soap operas on television. Sometimes Jesse would be in her playpen, sometimes Mary would cuddle her. Again, Jesse did not seem to have a preference.

For supper Jesse had more milk and Mary would have another sandwich, or would indulge in some spaghetti or a casserole. As usual, Jesse would show no interest in anything Mary fixed for herself.

When the typical day became too boring for Mary to endure any longer, she would go out to a movie, or go to the mall or go to the library. At first she was afraid that Jesse would pick a day at the library or the movies to let out with her first wail. But that never happened.

Times were easier when Joe was home. He could stay at the house and baby-sit while Mary went to play bridge or scrabble. But he was only home one week a month. Mary's lady friends were curious as to why Mary stayed away so long at a time. Mary didn't have an answer.

One morning at breakfast Mary was having fried eggs. As usual she absent mindedly dipped her finger in the yolk and put it in Jesse's mouth. Instead of just sucking the egg off, Jesse bit down – hard.

"Ouch!" Mary yelled as she attempted to extract her finger. "Let go of me!" she ordered. "I'm *not* food."

Her finger came out easily, but there was a tiny drop of blood on it. Mary instinctively put the finger in her mouth. Then she remembered where it had been and quickly removed it. Jesse just lay in her lap calmly watching the whole scene.

Mary reached down and gently opened Jesse's mouth. There, instead of just pink gums, were several pale, sharp-pointed teeth beginning to emerge. "Well," Mary thought to herself, " this is new!" She also recalled her original fantasy about Jesse being a cannibal. This time she didn't just shrug it off. She would have to be careful!

The next time Mary offered Jesse a bottle of water, Jesse spit out the tip of the nipple and proceeded to chug the water somewhat messily. Mary suddenly paid more attention to how Jesse was holding the bottle. She was holding it in the air using both hands and was having no trouble with it at all. Mary went to the kitchen, got a small plastic cup, put some water in it and returned to the playpen.

Mary took the bottle from Jesse. She leaned her up against the wall of the crib and handed her the cup, placing her hands securely around it. Jesse drank out of the cup like she had been doing it all her life. Then she dropped the cup onto the floor of the playpen, spilling the remaining contents. "Well," Mary thought, as she cleaned up the spill, "that's a first step."

At lunch, Mary helped Jesse drink out of a cup. Doing her best to ensure that the cup was not just thrown on the floor when Jesse had her fill. She used a small demitasse spoon to feed Jesse her yogurt. Jesse adapted very quickly. It would be a while before she could feed herself, but she was well on the way.

A few days later, Mary was surprised when she came into the living room and found Jesse sitting up against the wall of the playpen. Mary shook her head in wonder. She knew she had laid Jesse down on the floor of the crib as she always did. It came to Mary that perhaps Jesse had learned just from her drinking lesson. "If that were the case," she wondered, "what else might she learn? And what else might she already know?"

Mary was sure that Jesse had grown. She did not wear clothes so there was nothing for her to grow out of, but she just looked a bit larger. Mary got a tape measure from her sewing box, stretched Jesse out on the floor of the playpen and measured her. She was some eighteen inches long.

When Joe returned from his current run, he was surprised at how much Jesse had changed. She was now sitting up most of the time, drinking out of her cup and handling toys placed within her reach. She still hadn't made a sound, but Mary and Joe waited with great anticipation – and dread – the day that she started.

With Joe back, Mary went shopping for some toys for Jesse. Mary had no idea what Jesse might like. The 'age appropriate' labels on the various products were of little help. Mary did not know how old Jesse actually was. Combined with no knowledge as to how fast she was growing, it was a losing proposition. Mary finally settled for a couple of stuffed animals – a horse and a lamb – and a couple of baby books and wooden puzzles. She decided she would start there and see what developed.

Just as Mary was leaving the toy store she bumped into an old friend, Sheila Brady. Mary used to play bridge and scrabble with Sheila on a regular basis. Mary steeled herself for the impact.

"Oh hello, Mary," Sheila began. "I've really missed you at bridge for the past three months. You know how the ladies talk; there have already been some delicious rumors. What in the world has been going on?"

"Hi, Sheila. There is really nothing wrong. I just haven't been able to get out of the house as much lately."

"Does that have anything to do with children's toys?" Sheila thought she had a major find and was going in for the kill.

"I was just buying a few gifts for one of Joe's relatives. He doesn't know anything about shopping for babies."

"And you do?" Sheila queried. "Besides, I thought that you and Joe were only children ..."

"Black sheep side of the family," Mary hastily explained. "Sorry, Sheila, I've got to be going." And with that Mary fled from the scene.

The toys were not a big hit at the start. When Mary gave Jesse the stuffed horse, she looked at it, felt it, tasted it and then ignored it. She seemed to like the lamb. At least she didn't throw it across the playpen. She set it down next to her and took it to bed with her that night.

The puzzle appeared to be beyond Jesse's ability at the moment. Mary showed her how to dump the parts onto the playpen floor and then put them back into the frame. Jesse was adept at dumping the parts, but was not interested in reinserting them.

The little book was made of heavy cardboard, supposedly immune to baby saliva. Mary sat with Jesse in her lap and 'read' it to her, showing her the pretty pictures of the farm animals. That also seemed to pique Jesse's interest. But it was really hard to tell because she essentially remained as stoic as ever.

Joe enjoyed playing with Jesse when he was home, but he was so seldom at home. When he set off across country again, Mary's depression returned. She also enjoyed playing with Jesse, but doing housework and taking care of Jesse just wasn't what she was used to. It was definitely not what she wanted. It had been almost six months now; Mary was ready for some excitement.

And Mary got that excitement. She stopped by a thrift shop on one of her grocery shopping trips and picked up a little potty chair. It was made of green plastic and had a little seat above a removable pot. Mary had never seen Jesse urinate, but she supposed Jesse did it pretty much the same way she did.

Mary checked the bottom of the playpen to ensure that it was watertight. Then she placed the potty chair in the playpen. She removed Jesse's diaper and noticed that it was still dry. She picked up Jesse and placed her on the potty chair. Jesse wobbled a bit, but finally settled. Mary picked up a cup of water that she had hidden from Jesse and poured some of it noisily into the chamber pot from the rear. Then she waited.

After five minutes, Mary poured a little more water into the potty. Mary hoped that the noise would register and trigger the proper response. Eventually, Mary ran out of water and Jesse still had not contributed a drop. The noise of the pouring water had elicited a response in Mary, however. She needed a trip to the bathroom.

Mary refused to pass up a chance to educate Jesse. So she picked up Jesse and carried her into the bathroom. There, Mary placed Jesse on the floor facing the toilet, pulled down her own pants and squatted over the toilet bowl, making sure that Jesse could see what was happening. Mary's urine flowed out noisily into the toilet. "See," Mary pointed out. "That's how it's done."

Mary picked up Jesse and returned her to the playpen. She gathered the empty water glass and the pot from the potty chair and went to the kitchen. When she returned to pick up the potty chair, surprisingly, a small amount of liquid spilled out the open back. Mary just stared at Jesse, who was still sitting where Mary had left her in the center of the playpen. Then Mary went to get a rag to clean up the spill. She decided that she would settle for boring a while longer.

Chapter 7

What Social Life?

Before Jesse's arrival, Mary had a full social calendar. While Joe was out on the road, she would go to the Unitarian-Universalist church on Sunday, play Bridge on Monday and Wednesday, play Scrabble on Thursday, go to a philosophy club on Saturday and fit in various luncheons and book clubs in between.

When Jesse appeared on the scene, all of these events suddenly went away. Mary had to stay home to care for Jesse. She couldn't take Jesse with her – that would have exposed her to a bevy of potential gossips. There was no one she could call on to baby-sit – all of her and Joe's relatives lived out of state.

After the meeting with Sheila, when Mary didn't show up for Bridge on Monday, her friends were on the phone asking if something were wrong. Mary reassured them that all was well and she was just taking a break. The same question popped up from all of her other activities. And Mary gave each inquirer the same answer. After the fourth or fifth call, Mary was beginning to sense her sudden limitations. Then the calls just stopped coming.

At first Mary was infatuated with baby Jesse. She could hold her, feed her, change her diaper. Mary enjoyed playing the role of mother; this was likely to be her only chance. Mary also enjoyed her friends and her life of freedom. She continued to search for some way to merge the two lifestyles, but she always came up empty.

So long as Jesse fit into the swaddling wrap and the sling, she was hidden from any casual observation. Mary could safely take her out shopping or to the movies. She just had to be careful to avoid any of her friends who would want a closer look at the new baby.

Mary started looking for other interesting activities. She started watching television shows. She could put Jesse in her play pen and settle back with a cup of coffee or tea and watch quiz shows, soap operas, the afternoon movie, news shows. There was a pretty good selection. At least that was what Mary initially thought. After watching television for a few days, Mary began to realize why television was being called a wasteland. It was really mind numbing when taken in large doses.

Mary tried clearing off the dining room table and laying out a jigsaw puzzle. She could be active – constantly moving around the table. It was mentally stimulating. It provided a sense of accomplishment when the puzzle finally came together. But it wasn't fun.

Mary even tried going to a gym. She put Jesse in a large gym bag and set off for the local Y. She looked a little weird toting the gym bag between machines, but she had a good workout. Mary eventually decided that exercise was good in limited doses, but too much exercise was as mind numbing as too much television. To her credit, Mary did try jogging, but done in the cool of the morning it cut into her sleeping time and in the middle of the day it was suicidally hot.

Mary's problem was that she just missed socializing with her friends. She could find no substitute for sharing the latest gossip while engaging in some sort of a mental challenge.

Because of her lack of socializing, Mary especially looked forward to Joe's monthly return. They had always had a robust sex life and now Mary needed that even more that usual. Joe on the other hand, was not sure what to make of her more insistent and more frequent advances. At first, it was enjoyable, but as Mary's demands increased Joe began to be worn down. He started gently resisting sex twice a day every day. Then he began finding other things that required his immediate attention. This caused different sparks to fly between Mary and Joe.

One day, while Joe was out on the road, and Mary was doing her weekly shopping, she noticed an attractive ad in the store for a particular brand of wine. Mary wasn't quite sure what to make of it. She had never consumed alcohol in any great amount. She wasn't even a social drinker. But she was looking for something to improve her life, and that ad seemed to say that this wine was the solution. Mary decided to try a bottle. She was very glad when the check-out clerk put the bottle in a separate paper bag.

That afternoon, Mary plopped down on the sofa with a glass of wine instead of her usual cup of tea. The wine was cool and sweet. It took the edge off Mary's ennui. It also added to the overall mind numbing. But that glass of wine really hit the spot. Mary considered indulging in a second glass, but decided against it. Maybe tomorrow …

A glass of wine did indeed become a staple of afternoon television. Never more than one glass, Mary firmly insisted. It just took a little of the edge off and enabled her to get through the day without her friends.

When Joe was home, Mary made sure that there were no bottles of wine anywhere in the house. Her wine glass was carefully washed and dried and put back in the china cupboard. Mary didn't realize that she was at the top of a very slippery slope.

Chapter 8

She Walks; She Talks

Life progressed by little steps through the summer months. Jesse had a new favorite food: mushrooms. She had smelled then when Mary was making some spaghetti sauce and acted as though she was interested. Mary made the mistake of giving her a mushroom that was covered with sauce. It immediately came flying out of Jesse's mouth and halfway across the kitchen.

"I'm sorry, baby," Mary exclaimed. She took another mushroom to the sink and washed it off. "Here, try this," she offered the clean mushroom. Jesse scarfed down the mushroom and looked for more. By the time she was satisfied, Jesse had eaten most of the mushrooms in the sauce.

Once her teeth had come in, Jesse also developed a taste for cheese of all sorts. But not the cheese 'product' as Mary learned when Jesse sent a glob of product sailing across the table at Joe.

Jesse could feed herself, now. She had no trouble using the potty chair and was almost tall enough to use the toilet, but she still hadn't given any real indication that she could walk. She gave every indication that she understood simple words, but she also remained stubbornly mute.

Wednesday had become shopping days at the Carpenter household and Mary was about to set out on this weekly duty. Jesse had already grown too large to fit in the original baby sling. But Mary did not want to carry her openly, so she had created a new, larger sling. She could then wrap her securely in swaddling cloth and slip the resulting covered bundle securely into the new sling.

Mary carried the swaddling wrap and the sling to the playpen where Jesse was sitting. She spread out the swaddling wrap and picked up Jesse to set her in the middle of it. Jesse looked up at her and very clearly said, "Dondo dat! I don likit!"

Mary recoiled in absolute shock. For a minute she just stared at Jesse. Then she thought to close her mouth. Jesse's speech wasn't clear, but her meaning was perfectly clear. "You can talk," was the best Mary could offer.

"I know ... some ... words," Jesse said. She paused between words because it sometimes took her a few seconds to call up the proper word.

"How long have you been able to talk?" Mary did not know why she asked such a question, it just seemed relevant at the moment.

"I donno ... a while."

Mary continued to sit on the floor by the play pen. Her thoughts were racing. Her "conversations" with Jesse had consisted mostly of "baby talk", ma-ma, da-da, horsey, din-din and the like. It slowly became obvious to Mary that Jesse had been learning to speak from the television shows she had been watching every day. As this thought dawned, Mary slowly turned her gaze toward the TV set. Jesse also turned her gaze toward the TV.

Mary's paranoia, which had been in remission for the past couple of months, suddenly kicked up a notch. If Jesse was smart enough to learn how to speak English on her own, what else was she capable of doing? How much did she know that she wasn't letting on?

After a few minutes, Mary managed to collect her thoughts. Looking at Jesse, she asked, "Can you understand what I am saying?"

"Yes." Jesse's voice was tiny, but clear.

"If you don't understand what I am saying, will you tell me?"

"Yes."

"Can you walk about the play pen?"

"Yes."

"Show me ... please."

Jesse was on her feet in one simple move, faster than Mary could comprehend. Then she walked with ease around the play pen. Jesse stopped on the side where Mary was sitting and held on to the top rail to steady herself as she wobbled a bit on the well-padded bottom.

Mary was confused by Jesse's initial agility and her final wobbling. She decided that Jesse was just learning to walk and did not present a problem, yet.

"I have a problem, Jesse," Mary explained carefully. "I need to go out shopping. You won't fit in the sling unless you are in the swaddling wrap. I can't put you in the stroller, because I don't have any clothes for you."

"Why ... need ... clothes?"

Mary hesitated. How could she explain the situation? "If people can see what you look like, it could cause all of us harm."

"Why?"

"Because, you don't look like we do. You know that you and I are different..."

"I am ... young. Will I not ... change ... as I get ...older?"

"I don't know, Jesse. But you do not look like I did when I was your age. And your appearance would cause other people to ask embarrassing, and dangerous, questions. That is why you can't be seen, either outside the house or through the windows. Do you understand me?"

"I think I ... understand ... your words," Jesse answered, but it was obvious to Mary that she really was thinking, "But ... I ... still ... don't know ... why."

"Trust me, it just is," was the best that Mary could manage.

"You ... can ... go. I stay here."

Mary wasn't comfortable with that idea. She could conjure up all sorts of problems that might arise if she left Jesse alone and unsupervised, especially now that she knew Jesse could move about. On the other hand ...

"If I let you stay here alone, will you promise not to leave the play pen? I will be back before lunch."

"I don ... understand ... 'promise'."

"Will you still be in the play pen when I get back?"

"Yes."

Mary still wasn't sure she was doing the right thing, but she could see no other alternative. She could force Jesse into the swaddling clothes, but that could lead to real trouble. What if Jesse decided to get vocal while they were out in a public place? In the end, Mary added a word – library – to her grocery list, said good-bye to Jesse had headed out the door.

In fact, Mary had made a great error. She had not yet figured out that Jesse was a very literal being. When Mary changed, 'promise to stay in …' into 'still be in …', she changed the whole meaning of her statement in Jesse's mind.

Jesse was still standing at the side of the play pen when Mary went out the door. She listened until she heard Mary start the car in the driveway and drive off down the block. Then Jesse stretched. It felt good to be on her own. She wandered around the play pen, teetering every once in a while on the soft floor. Even with the television set on, this was terribly boring.

Joe and Mary's house was an incredibly complex and fascinating place to Jesse. There were so many interesting gadgets. She knew what some of them did, but others were a complete mystery. It was, she decided, time to solve some of the mysteries.

Jesse grabbed hold of the top rail of the play pen and vaulted over it. At first she just wandered about the house. She looked into each room, some she knew, others she had never been inside. She discovered drawers and cabinets and opened each in turn. Some things she recognized, some, like a pair of scissors and a pair of pliers, she could intuit from simple examination. Other items were a complete mystery. Jesse had seen Mary using a knife. Jesse defined a knife as a handle attached to a sharp blade. When Jesse found a similar object with a long grooved handle attached to a round blade, it did not make any sense. What could it possibly cut? And there were several other strange objects in a drawer with the pliers.

The television set also attracted Jesse's attention. It seemed to have an unending supply of pictures. Jesse noted that there were two wires attached to the television set and that it was warm to the touch. There were also several control knobs identified by some of the same strange symbols she had seen displayed on the screen. She had a thought: tele-vision – tele-phone. Maybe they were similar. She went over to the telephone and looked at it. More of the strange symbols. But only one wire was connected to it. A wire that looked similar to one of the wires attached to the television set. The telephone was not warm to the touch.

Another thought occurred. Jesse went into the kitchen. There on the counter was a thing that Mary often used when she was making breakfast. It also had a wire attached to it. That wire was similar to one on the television set. Jesse pressed the lever that she had seen Mary press. The thing began to get warm. Jesse waited. For a few minutes nothing happened. Then wisps of smoke and a strange odor emanated from the thing. Jesse could see a orange glow inside it. At this point Jesse began to be afraid. She grabbed the lever and tried to push it back where it had initially been. It wasn't easy, but she made it. The orange glow and the heat subsided.

Jesse went back to the living room. There was a lamp behind one of the chairs that had a similar wire attached to it. Jesse looked closely and saw what was probably a switch. She turned the switch and the light came on. She felt the light and found that it was getting warm. Afraid of more smoke, she turned the switch until the light went out. Jesse had learned about switches, about the use of strange symbols and that one type of wire caused things to get warm.

There were people sounds outside the house. Jesse followed the sounds and went to a convenient window. She looked out at the neighborhood for the first time unfettered by swaddling clothes or sling. There were some young children playing in the yard across the street. They were running and laughing and having a good time. Jesse sat and watched them. She had a sudden desire to be out there with them. Before she could devise a way to join them, she saw Mary's car approaching and heard it stop in the driveway. Jesse jumped up, ran across the room and leaped into the playpen just as Mary came in the front door.

Mary carried a bag of groceries into the kitchen and set it on the counter. A strange, but familiar odor attracted her attention: burnt toast. Mary felt the toaster. It was warm, but there were no telltale crumbs of bread anywhere on the counter. Mary turned toward the living room, then hesitated. What was she going to say? Jesse, have you been making toast? The very thought was ludicrous. Jesse didn't eat bread! Instead, Mary put the groceries away and vowed to say nothing about the toaster. But she would be watching Jesse much more closely in the future. Mary's paranoia began to simmer again.

When Mary returned to the living room, Jesse was sitting quietly in her playpen, just as though nothing had happened. Mary went over to the couch near the playpen and sat down. "I'm proud of you, Jesse," she began. "You were right here in your playpen when I returned." She watched Jesse closely and thought she saw just a glimmer concerning what was not said.

"You are growing up, Jesse," Mary said. "Perhaps we need to talk about what your new needs might be."

"I ... need ... learn. I ... need ... outside."

"But, I've already explained. You can't go outside where you could be seen by others. As for learning, that we can work on."

"I am ... prisoner?" It was as much a question as a statement of fact.

"Oh, no, Jesse!" Mary struggled to find the right words. "We are just trying to protect you from your enemies. Let me think about what we can do."

Neither Mary nor Jesse was happy. They each planned to be more careful in the future.

That night, Jesse was standing in her crib looking out at the brightly moonlit night. Her crib had been moved over to the wall under the window when the bassinet had been removed. How she wanted to be outside! She looked out the window at the back yard. She saw the tool shed just to the left of her window. She looked at the window. She tried to open it, but it wouldn't open. She noticed the lock and examined it. A few seconds later the window was open. There was no screen on her window, so it was simple for Jesse to climb up on the side of the crib, climb out onto the window ledge and jump over to the top of the shed. From that location it was an easy jump up to the roof.

The walls of the adobe-style house extended up beyond the roof level. Once she was on the roof, Jesse could not be seen from below. She lay down and just gazed at the heavens. She did not know that the lights up there – the ones that weren't moving – were stars. She just enjoyed the enchanting beauty of the millions of little blinking lights. Jesse spent the entire night on the roof

It was not until the sun began to rise that Jesse remembered she was not supposed to be outside the house. She quickly jumped up, dropped to the shed roof and on to the windowsill. She had just landed in her crib when she knew she was in trouble.

"Good morning!" Mary was standing in the middle of Jesse's room. She was definitely not happy. "Just where have you been – or should I even waste my time asking?"

"I was … up on the roof. It was … wonderful!" Jesse was bubbling over. Then she remembered that she was expected to be contrite. "No one saw me," she whispered.

Mary realized that was probably true, but they really couldn't take the chance. She simply closed and locked the window.

Chapter 9

Jessie's New World

Mary went to the kitchen to fix breakfast for Jesse and herself. As she was standing at the counter, she looked out the window into the back yard. She and Joe had put in a small patio by the back door, but had never done anything to improve the yard. It consisted of sand sparsely populated with a few small cacti. She had a clear view of their neighbor's house.

Mary stopped preparing breakfast. She just stood there looking out the window. Something was bothering her about that yard. It was a big open space that she and Joe had never used. What about it was so important? There was certainly not enough room for an alien space ship to land. Mary laughed a little nervously at the thought. Then it came to her. She turned and ran back into the living room.

"Jesse, " Mary asked excitedly, "if you had a small space outside that could be your own, would that be enough, or would you get bored with it and want even more?"

"Bored? I don't ... understand."

"'Bored' means it doesn't interest you, doesn't excite you."

"Will I ... have ... other children ... to ... play with?"

"No," Mary tried to sound caring but strict. "Until we can find more of your people, you will have to settle for Joe and me."

That did not make Jesse jump for joy. "I …
would … enjoy … being outside – even … by
myself," Jesse conceded.

Mary went back to finish breakfast and think
some more about her idea. That afternoon, she
went to work. First she picked up Jesse and
carried her back to her room and placed he in her
crib. Jesse was a little agitated over this
innovation, until Mary told her to stand there and
look out the window.

Mary went out to the back yard. Joe kept a
small storage shed in the back yard next to Jesse's
window. As Mary approached it she waved to
Jesse. It seemed to Mary that Joe had a measuring
gizmo out here left over from the patio
construction. She poked around. There was the
grill, rake, broom, shovel, blower, shelves with
various tools. Then, hidden back in a corner, was
her goal: a wheel with a handle attached to it and
a counter to register the distance the wheel
traveled.

Mary extracted the device and went back into
the yard and looked around, getting the lay of the
land as it were. Satisfied with what she saw, she
went over to the corner of the house by the shed,
reset the counter on the measuring device, placed
the wheel at the corner of the house and started
walking slowly to the back end of their property.

Pulling a piece of paper and a pen out of her
pants pocket, Mary wrote down the measurement.
Then she reset the counter and walked across the
back property line until she was opposite the far
corner of the house. Again, she wrote down the
measurement, reset the counter and walked back
to the corner of the house by the street. When she
had recorded the measurement, she returned the

device to the storage shed and went back inside to Jesse.

"You saw what I did? Mary said. "I was measuring the back yard. How would you like it if you could go out there and play whenever you wanted?"

"Yes! I would … like it!"

"You can't do that yet! Mary apologized. "And I can't promise anything. But I am going to do my best to make that happen. You will just have to wait until Joe gets back. Okay?"

"Okay." Jesse was thrilled with the idea. But Jesse was not thrilled by having to wait. When Jesse wanted something, she wanted it – now!

Mary lifted Jesse out of her crib and placed her on the floor. Jesse got the idea and went back to the living room. Instead of jumping into the playpen, she climbed up onto the sofa and settled down to watch the afternoon soap operas.

Armed with the measurements, Mary went into Joe's den and sat down with the phone and the phonebook. At first she started with a couple of fencing companies, just getting the cost of some plain wood fencing about six-foot tall. She also checked on the price of chain link fencing. That was cheaper, until you added the slats that would be required to block out onlookers. It wasn't looking good. She checked their bank balance. She pulled out the checkbook and started making notes of necessary bills. If Joe was on schedule, he should be calling that night or the next. Mary wanted to be ready.

When Joe called, he and Mary exchanged some preliminary amenities, then Joe asked, as he always did, how things were going at home. Mary told him of the problem with Jesse and her proposed solution. At first, Joe did not like the idea at all. He didn't relish the idea of a fence, and he really didn't like the cost. He was doing his best to build up a retirement account and a fence would dig a big hole in that account. They talked for most of an hour. Joe wanted to postpone a decision until he got home. Mary argued that if they did that, they might not be able to get the fence up before Joe had to go back on the road. Finally, Joe gave in and told Mary to order the necessary supplies – and he gave her a basic list of what would be required.

The next day, Mary was back on the phone with various suppliers arguing for a good price. Once she found the lowest price, she set delivery for Monday a week away. Then Mary got a scathingly brilliant idea. She started calling toy stores until she found what she was looking for. It would add less than $100 to the total. It would also be delivered on Monday.

Joe pulled in as usual on Sunday night. After saying hello to Jesse and Mary and a quick meal, he went straight to bed. On Monday morning he awoke to shouting and unusual noises. He grudgingly pulled himself out of bed and wandered into the kitchen. Looking out the window he saw the cause of the noise. A large truck had pulled up at the side of the house and some men were using a forklift to unload fencing. Another, somewhat smaller, truck was also by the side of the house with more men unloading something into the back yard. The first thought that entered his mind was, What in the world have I got myself into?

After breakfast and a few cups of coffee, Joe went out to survey his backyard. Fencing, associated posts, cement, nails, gate, hardware, boards to hold the fence together, and ... He couldn't quite place that odd pile of boards. Mary joined him, "Shall we get started?"

"First things first!" was Joe's terse statement. He retrieved the measuring device and rechecked Mary's numbers. Satisfied that they were close enough, he got some twine, small sticks and a large square from the shed. He placed a stick at the corner of the house and tied the string to it. Then he had Mary take the string out to the end of the yard. Using the square, Joe made sure it was tight and in a straight line. Mary tied the string to another stick and pushed it into the ground. Then Joe and Mary repeated the process at the other corner of the yard and at the other side of the house.

Next, while Joe fastened the two end pieces to the house, Mary went to a rental company to get a posthole digger and a nail gun. Joe also made a call to a labor service to get three day-laborers for the next day. Joe was explicit in his demands: young, strong, no booze, no drugs, have their own transportation, on site at six AM. He promised $75 cash per man for the day.

When Mary returned, they dug the holes for the short fence segments that would abut the house. Joe attached the fence segments and mixed up a small bag of "Quik-Crete" to fill the postholes. After admiring their work, Joe went in and ordered a portable potty. All was in readiness for the next day.

That night, Joe paid their neighbors a visit. He told them that he was in the process of building a fence around his yard. He intended to put the fence on his side of the property line. He gave them an option. If they paid half the cost of the fence between their respective properties, he would give them permission to connect to it, should they ever desire to put up a fence. Otherwise, he said he would put his fence just shy of the property line and they would not be able to use it. They said they would think it over.

The next morning Joe and Mary were up early. Mary roused Jesse and hung a sheer curtain over Jesse's window. She cautioned Jesse that she could watch, but to make sure she stayed far enough away from the window that she could not be seen from the outside.

The crew actually arrived on time. Joe organized them and in no time they were moving the fence sections into place along the string line. Then they stood up each section and marked the locations for the postholes. They took turns digging postholes, positioning the fence sections and connecting them with support members. By noon they had almost finished the back section and by late afternoon everything but the gate was in place. While the crew picked up the empty bags of Quik-Crete and put them in the garbage can, Joe put the hardware on the gate and laid the threshold. Twenty minutes later the gate was in place and functioning. A few minutes after that Joe had paid off the crew and sent them on their way.

Jesse was ready to run out and enjoy her new space, but the job was still not finished. After a good, long night's sleep. Joe and Mary were back at it. Joe went to return the nail gun and rent a paint sprayer. He stopped at the pain store for some wood sealer. The two of them spent that morning putting sealer on their new fence. The afternoon involved Mary's special purchase. It was a wooden swing set. Mary raked a large area in the center of the yard to even it out and remove any leftover cacti. Joe bolted the swing set braces together and attached the crossbar to one end. It was all the two of them could do to set that end upright. Then they had to raise it and hold it in place with a ladder while they jockeyed the other end close enough to be bolted in place. It was almost nightfall when they had all the other pieces hung. There were a simple swing, a glider, a slide and a hanging bar.

The last item, a swimming pool, was left until the next day. When Joe and Mary came back in for supper, and a well earned rest, they impressed on Jesse that there were still too many fumes from the sealant for it to be safe for her to go out in the yard. Tomorrow it would be all hers.

The next morning, Joe and Mary just stood back and watched as Jesse took off into her new world. She appeared to be a creature possessed. Running, leaping, even laughing? Jesse tried out everything. Joe and Mary were stunned when she ran up one of the swing set supports, along the crossbar and leaped from the other end, landing lightly on her feet. "She's just like a cat," Mary observed. Joe cautioned Jesse about the remaining cacti. He took her over to one of them and had her lightly touch the spines. She immediately grasped the necessity of giving them a wide berth. Mary found a place for the swimming pool and began filling it. She decided to limit the initial fill to about three feet. Considering Jesse's agility, she didn't think that should prove too dangerous.

Mary went inside to fix Joe's breakfast. She wondered if she would ever get Jesse out of the yard.

As for Joe, he still had work to do. He had to pick up the leftover wood, store the usable pieces in the shed with the extra nails and dispose of the rest. He wondered about relocating the garbage can from the kitchen door to outside the fence. Then decided to leave it; it had wheels, and Mary could move it once a week for pickup. He surveyed the yard for any other needs. Jesse was standing in the center of the yard looking at the swing set. She looked over at him and said just one word, "How?"

Joe smiled at her. Then he walked over and placed her in the seat of the swing. He got behind her and pushed, gently at first, then faster and harder. After a short ride, Joe stopped the swing and motioned Jesse to get off. Then he sat down and showed her how to start the swing and how to pump with her legs.

Next came the glider. Jesse figured out how to sit on it, but was temporarily baffled as to how to get it started. Her legs did not reach the ground. Joe pointed out the lever between her legs. He demonstrated what happened when it was pushed or pulled. Soon Jesse was gliding back and forth with ease.

The slide was another problem. Jesse's bare skin stuck to the slide and she didn't move an inch. The slide also became very hot sitting out in the summer sun. Joe thought for a moment. Then he went over to the pool, which was almost full by now, took the hose out. He went to the faucet and turned down the flow to a trickle and then lodged the hose in place at the top of the slide.

The trickling water cooled the slide and provided the necessary lubrication for a quick descent. Joe showed Jesse how to turn the water on and off and reminded her only to turn it on when she wanted to slide and to be sure to turn it off afterward.

Mary yelled that breakfast was ready and the two of them headed into the house. At the last minute, Jesse remembered and ran over to turn off the water.

Chapter 10

The ABC's of TV

Jesse's first and most pressing need had been met. Before turning her attention to Jesse's second need, Mary had a few needs of her own that had to be satisfied. Up to this point, Joe had been too exhausted to devote any time to Mary. Neither did he have any time to really relax since he had been home. He was just as virile as any other thirty-year-old, and was steadfastly faithful to Mary, but at the moment sex was the last thing on his mind. The best he could do was give her a quick kiss and the promise of things to come. Then he disappeared behind the closed door of his den to work on paying for the fence and slide set.

Mary took a cup of coffee into the living room and consulted the TV magazine. She considered the children's programs: *Sesame Street*, the *Electric Company*, *Mr. Rogers' Neighborhood*, the *Mickey Mouse Club*. She wanted to find out just what the various programs the local stations had to offer. Obviously, Jesse had learned some English just from watching TV. Would a specific set of programs offer something better.

The more Mary scanned the TV magazine, the more certain she became that there was nothing on TV at this time that would suit Jesse's need. *Sesame Street* was too simple, *Electric Company* was too advanced – at this time. The others were fine programs, but they emphasized social interaction and that was the last thing Mary wanted Jesse exposed to. She didn't see anything else that even came close.

Mary did some house cleaning and fixed lunch. Joe came out of his den to eat a bite, grab an extra soft drink and return to the den. Whenever Mary asked a question or made a comment, Joe just mumbled darkly about never being able to retire at this rate. Jesse was still enjoying her yard. She came in, grabbed some cheese and went back outside.

After lunch, Mary gave up. She knocked on the door of the den, opened it and told Joe that she was going to join her friends for their weekly Scrabble game. It had been a long time since she had had a day out. She reminded Joe to watch Jesse. Mary changed into a neat shirtdress, combed out her hair and took off.

Everyone at the scrabble game was glad to see Mary. They all had a question or two to ask: Where had she been? Had she been ill? Why hadn't she been coming? Mary did her best to give non-committal answers. At first all the concern was flattering, but when her answers proved unsatisfactory, the constant questioning became annoying. Mary just wanted to play scrabble and catch up on the gossip about others.

When the scores were tallied, Mary had not done as well as she usually did. The afternoon out had not lived up to her expectations. The women were discussing where to go for dinner, when Mary just quietly slipped out the door. Dinner would only have meant more time for questions without the benefit of any mental stimulation. She could find that at home.

Mary had great difficulty convincing Jesse to come from the yard that evening. Eventually, hunger and the promise that tomorrow would be another day to enjoy her yard was enough to get Jesse to come in. After dinner everyone settled down in the living room around the television set. At least Joe had some good news.

"It took all day to work up the numbers," he said, "but I talked to the bank late this afternoon and they are going to cover the cost of the back yard and tack the payments onto our mortgage."

Speaking of their mortgage always bothered Mary, "Won't that mean refinancing the house?" she asked.

"No," Joe explained. "They are giving us a separate loan, so the mortgage stays the same. It's just going to cost us an extra $50 per month. I think we can handle that without sacrificing too much. They're putting the money in our savings account to offset the money I pulled out to pay for the project."

After a couple of TV shows, Mary was ready to call it a night. Surprisingly, no one argued in the least. Jesse went straight to her room. Mary and Joe headed for their room. Mary said she wanted to take a quick shower. When she returned to the bedroom wearing her sexiest negligee, Joe was already snoring. Mary cried herself to sleep.

On Friday, Mary made a bargain with Jesse. Jesse could play out in the yard in the morning, but afternoons were going to be devoted to learning. Mary reminded Jesse that was one of her original needs; she reluctantly agreed. The learning would begin that afternoon. Mary spent the morning on the computer printing out some visual aids for her first lessons.

Mary devoted that afternoon to explaining the alphabet to Jesse. Her visual aids demonstrated upper and lower cases, printed versus script letters, and italics. Below each of the upper case letters Mary had printed the name of the letter. Mary spent the entire afternoon drilling Jesse on the order and pronunciation of the letters. By supper time she had it down pat.

This did not surprise Mary. She had almost come to expect that sort of reaction from Jesse. But Mary was worried. Human children took a year to master what Jesse had picked up, mostly on her own, in a matter of weeks. She thought back on the TV programs for children she had seen. They would only show one or two letters a day. What, Mary wondered, was Jesse's true capability? Like any young child, Jesse obeyed now out of a sense of … love? But what might happen as she grew older? For some reason, Mary didn't want to think about that.

Saturday morning Mary started the washing. Then she left Joe in charge and took off for the city library. The college library was fine for academic studies, but not for what Mary had in mind. She just hoped that the children's section had not been updated in a while. Unfortunately, the library, like children's television, was more show and glitz that it was substance. And Mary wanted substance.

When she couldn't find what she wanted at the library, Mary made the rounds of some good used book stores. After much walking and searching, Mary found a treasure trove: five "Big Little Books".

That afternoon Jesse got her first taste of the finest in children's literature.

"Today," Mary announced as she and Jesse settled down on the couch together to start their afternoon session, "we are going to read a book together. The title of this book is, 'Dick Tracy meets Flattop'. Dick Tracy was a police officer and Flattop was a criminal. This story tells how Dick Tracy captures Flattop and puts him in jail." Mary showed Jesse the color picture on the cover. Then she opened the book.

"See," she announced displaying the book, "there is a picture on this page that indicates what is happening. Now, watch my finger ..." With that Mary started reading the text, moving her finger under each word as she read it. Mary did not read especially slowly, but showed as much emotion as she could and matched her reading to the action. If she came to a word Jesse did not recognize, or could not figure out; or there was a situation that Jesse did not understand, Mary would stop and explain it. By supper time they had finished the book. Mary had been watching Jesse as she read. She noted that by the end of the book, Jesse was reading most of the words right along with her.

When she went to the kitchen to fix supper, Mary was quite satisfied with her efforts. Jesse actually stayed on the couch with the book until she was called to eat.

That night Mary had to finish the washing and get Joe ready to hit the road again on Sunday. By the time she got to bed, Joe was again sleeping soundly. Mary almost dumped the last load of folded clothes on top of him just out of spite. Perhaps the way he was treating her was just his reaction to Jesse's presence. For the second night in a row, Mary cried herself to sleep.

Chapter 11

Reading, Writing, Arithmetic

With Joe back on the road, Jesse and Mary resumed their classes. Jesse could read fluently now, even though her vocabulary was still somewhat limited. So Mary started in on arithmetic and the concept of numbers. Mary had studied computer data processing when she was in school, never imagining then that she would ever have occasion to put it in practice. Now it seemed it would come in handy indeed.

Mary's first endeavor was to teach Jesse how to compute in binary. There were only two digits to keep track of, so Jesse quickly grasped the concept of positional notation. She also quickly became adept at addition and inversion. With those skills she could add, subtract, multiply and divide at will.

Then Mary gave Jesse a simple chart

```
0:0000  +    2 + 1 = 3
1:0001  -    2 − 1 = 1
2:0010  *    2 * 2 = 4
3:0011  /    2 / 1 = 2
4:0100  =    2 = 2
5:0101  <    1 < 2
6:0110  >    2 > 1
7:0111  √    √4 = 2
8:1000  ()   ( 1 + 2 ) / 1 = 3
9:1001  .
```

and proceeded to teach her the decimal system.

That took a few days. Mary was constantly surprised at Jesse's ability to quickly absorb knowledge that would have taken an average human months to learn.

By the time Joe returned, Mary had almost exhausted both herself and her knowledge of arithmetic and Jesse was asking for more. Ever helpful, Joe suggested that Mary teach Jesse something else, perhaps geography. But it was Jesse who suggested a way out for everyone.

"Mary, when can you go back and get me some new books?" Jesse asked at breakfast one morning.

"What kind of books?" Mary asked casually as she scraped off some over done toast.

"I don't know ... " It was hard to ask for something specific when one didn't even know what the possibilities were.

"Have you looked at the library in Joe's den?" Mary was engaged in scrambling some over-easy eggs.

"Library?" Jesse asked.

"A collection of books." Mary sat down at the table with the remnants of her breakfast.

"I have looked at them, but they didn't inspire me," Jesse was nibbling on some cottage cheese. "I'd really like some more arithmetic books and perhaps some other sciences. But I won't really know until I have a chance to see them."

"Why don't you go to the library?" Joe offered. Jesse didn't quite understand what Joe was referring to, but she perked up and smiled.

Mary looked up incredulously, "Library!" she almost screamed. "Joe! How can you eve suggest that we do that? Jesse can't leave the house." Jesse's smile all but disappeared.

"Not alone, of course," Joe replied. "You'd have to take her. And she would have to have some decent clothes ..."

The conversation continued back and forth for some time. Joe trying his best to work out a solution, Mary was just as adamantly maintaining the whole idea was ridiculous and dangerous. Finally, Joe grew exasperated at Mary's stubbornness.

"Mary," he said sternly, "go get your cloth measuring tape." With Jesse standing in the middle of the kitchen, Joe used the tape and an old clothing catalogue to figure out what size she was. Joe dispatched Mary to procure some appropriate clothing and make-up for a young girl.

When Mary returned, Joe and Jesse played dress-up. Mary had procured a pair of opaque tights in dark blue, a long-sleeved white blouse with a high collar, tennis shoes, a pair of dark blue shorts and ... a wig. Jesse didn't mind the clothes, but the wig, made of shoulder-length light brown hair, was not a hit.

When Jesse was completely dressed, Mary applied a light brown foundation to Jesse's exposed skin. The end result, topped off with a pair of fashionable sunglasses, was a very acceptable young human. When Jesse saw herself in the full-length mirror in the hallway even she was amazed. Then she simply broke down laughing at the image.

The next day, Mary took a properly dressed Jesse to the local branch library. The library was located next to a community shopping area. It was a small brick building that had once been a convenience store. It had been enlarged and remodeled. Directly opposite the entrance was the librarian's desk where books were checked in and out. To the right of the entrance was the children's section with several low shelves and tables. Behind that were the library offices and storage area. To the left was a large card catalogue listing the libraries collection. To the front was the fiction section and to the rear the non-fiction section. Immediately to the left of the entrance was a closet in which the paperback mystery novels were stored. The librarian kept an eagle-eye out to ensure that no young people got into that closet with all the lurid paperback covers. Beyond the adult books an extra room had been added for meetings and lectures.

Mary took Jesse to the librarian and got her a library card. The librarian explained how to check out books initially limiting Jesse to two books per visit. Then Mary showed Jesse how to use the card catalogue to find a book and how to locate that book in the library. Jesse wasn't tall enough to view the top drawers of the catalogue, but she soon learned where and how the non-fiction books were stored.

That was all Jesse needed. She was in her element now. She moved quickly through the library, flitting from book to book. Mary just gave up and sat down in a convenient chair while Jesse browsed to her heart's content. After a couple of hours, she told Jesse it was time to leave and to select her books.

When Jesse had successfully checked out her books she and Mary left for home. Mary was definitely not ready for the next step.

The next step came in a few days, after Joe had once more set out on the road. Jesse asked Mary to take her to the library so she could return the books she had and get something else. That was the last thing Mary wanted to do and she said as much.

Jesse was not willing to accept that answer. Her independence had been ignited and she was not willing to go back to her previous status as a prisoner. She just nodded and went back to her room. A few minutes later she was dressed, made up and wigged. She grabbed her books and slipped quietly out the window into the back yard. She easily climbed over the fence, ripping the soles of her tights to shreds in the process, and took off down the street.

Jesse had made careful note of the route to the library. She was soon walking in the front door. She spent several hours in the library.

When Mary discovered that Jesse was missing, she couldn't believe it. She searched the house twice and the back yard three times before she grudgingly accepted that Jesse had flown the coop. Mary didn't doubt that Jesse had attempted to go to the library, but had she made it. Mary looked up the library's number. She picked up the phone and dialed the number. Then she hung up the phone. What would she say? Is my daughter there? What daughter? Maybe niece...? Yes,

Joe's niece. She dialed the number again. The phone just rang.

Mary looked at her watch. It was already three PM on Saturday; the library was closed. Where could Jesse be? Locked in the closed library? Wandering around the streets? Discovered and in the hands of the police? The only thing Mary knew for sure was that she couldn't call the police. Mary was pacing around the kitchen. She was getting too hyper to think clearly. She pulled a bottle of wine from the back of the pantry and poured and glass. She needed to calm down and think.

Mary did not hear Jesse returning. Jesse removed her clothes and make-up, stowed her books in her room and wandered out to the living room. Mary was asleep on the couch. Jesse wandered out to the kitchen for something to eat then went out to the yard to exercise and relax. When Mary woke up later, she found Jesse asleep in her room.

The next morning Mary tried desperately to scold Jesse for her actions the previous day. But Jesse was too wrapped up in a book about geography to pay any attention. Finally, Mary just told Jesse never to go out again without permission or she would call the police and have them pick Jesse up. That caused Jesse to look up for a second and then go back to her book.

Eventually, Jesse wore Mary down. Jesse had a problem. She was looking at maps that depicted the Earth as a flat surface, yet Jesse understood that the Earth was a planet, and planets were usually spherical. She asked Mary for help. Mary took a look at the book Jesse was reading. Then she handed Jesse a large piece of paper and told her to trace the outline of one of the maps on the paper and cut it out.

In a few minutes Jesse had the requested outline in hand. Mary took it from her and started bending it. To Jesse's astonishment, the bended paper slowly took the shape of a sphere. A few pieces of tape held it in shape. Then Mary explained the difference and the usefulness of polar and Mercator projections of the Earth's surface. One of the books had a picture of a student globe in it. Jesse asked if they could get one of those so that she could better understand the proportions of the planet. Mary groaned at the thought of the extra expense, but agreed to look into it.

When Joe returned from his tour, he found a new object had been added to his den. A large globe was adorning a corner of his desk. Joe thought that was delightful and enjoyed several hours explaining Great Circle Routes to Jesse. When he discovered that Jesse was perusing books on aviation, he drew the line. No airplanes!

Over the coming months Jesse spent more and more time at the library. She visited so often that the librarians recognized her and nodded to her as she came and went. When one of the librarians asked why she wasn't in school, Jesse simply said she was being home-schooled and was doing research for her homework. That seemed to satisfy everyone.

Mary resigned herself to Jesse's outings as long as she went directly to and from the library and spoke to no one. Whenever Jesse was out on her own, Mary kept her panic under control with a glass of wine.

Chapter 12

Touring America

It had been several years since Joe had brought Jesse home in swaddling clothes. She had grown to a grand height of almost four feet. Despite her almost innate ability to learn and apply factual information, Jesse had great difficulty appreciating size and distance. She studied the atlas and the globe diligently, but couldn't quite relate the difference in scale between the two. And she was completely baffled by the size of even her suburb of Tucson to the small area on the Arizona map devoted to the whole town and the fact that Tucson didn't even appear on the globe.

Jesse bugged Joe incessantly whenever he was home. He had explained to her several times about his job, driving trucks all over the States. How it took him three weeks to cover the country from coast to coast. Jesse had studied the road maps he had given her, she could name all of the states, she even knew all the state capitals. But the big picture continued to allude her.

Finally, as Joe, Mary and Jesse were sitting around the breakfast table, Joe could take it no longer. "Jesse, how would you like to really see this country – up close and personal?"

"Joe, no!" Mary exclaimed. "You can't take Jesse out on the road. She could be discovered."

"Nonsense, Mary," Joe tried to calm her down. "She'll have to stay in the cab, and hide in the sleeper when we are in a terminal. But no one will be able to get a good look at her while we're on the road. What do you think, Jesse?"

Jesse's sense of adventure had just shifted into overdrive. "I'd love it!"

"You don't mind having to hide out while we're in the terminals?"

"Not at all." Jesse was still excited by the whole idea.

"Joe, I still don't think this is a good idea. Too much could go wrong." Mary still hoped she could discourage Joe from taking the chance.

"Mary, I seem to remember that we had a lot of fun the time I took you out right after we were married." Joe was smiling at Mary. "Why don't we all go?"

"No," Mary responded. "Once was enough for me. If you insist on taking Jesse with you, I am definitely not going."

"Okay," Jesse agreed. "You can stay here and fix us a big meal when we return. When do we start?"

"We'll leave early Monday morning, as usual." Joe said. "Jesse, you bring your road atlas and the map of the United States. You'll also need some cans of mushrooms and some hard cheese and water. We won't have any refrigeration and stores will be few and far between. You understand?"

Jesse nodded.

"Oh, and you'd better bring along your usual clothes", Joe Suggested. "You won't need them in the truck, but better safe than sorry. Remember, we don't leave until Monday ..."

Jesse was already on the way to gather her belongings.

Joe roused Jesse right on schedule at four AM Monday morning. Mary was sleeping soundly, so the pair went quietly out to Joe's truck. Joe showed Jesse how to climb up and open the door on the passenger side of the truck. Jesse clambered up, none to steadily, and stowed her food and maps in a compartment in the sleeper. Then she settled into the passenger seat. Jesse had never gotten to see the inside of the truck before. She marveled at all the room in the truck and especially at all the gauges, levers, buttons and the huge steering wheel. She leaned over so she could see Joe's entire console.

Joe got in the driver's seat and stowed his logbook. Then he handed a small package to Jesse. "I have to record my travels in my logbook," he explained. "Here's a journal so you can record yours, and a camera so you can take pictures as we drive along. Now sit back and relax; we're on our way. First stop: the Tucson terminal."

Jesse watched carefully as Joe started the big diesel engine and slowly pulled the truck out of the yard and onto the road. It took them about ten minutes to wend their way along the back roads to the Trans National Trucking terminal. It was a huge square building surrounded by a tall chain-link fence and brightly lit in the early morning darkness.

As he approached the gate, Joe reached for one of the three microphones dangling above his head. "Truck 381 to dispatch," Joe said. The gate swung open and Joe pointed to a small box attached to the windshield. "Transponder. Opens the gates and identifies me to dispatch," Joe whispered to Jesse.

"381, Bay 23 left" came out of the radio. Joe acknowledged the message and turned the truck toward the left side of the terminal building. "Time to get in back," Joe told Jesse.

Even from the sleeper compartment Jesse could see a long dock running down the side of the building with large numbers posted every so often. There were trailers parked at some of the numbers, including number 23.

Joe swung the truck around and backed up to the trailer at bay number 23. "Stay there," he cautioned Jesse and climbed down out of the cab. Jesse could hear several strange sounds. The truck bounced a little. Then silence.

Joe returned in about ten minutes, threw his logbook into a crevice between the seats. He started out slowly and stopped to test the air brakes. When he was satisfied with the performance of the trailer he put the truck in gear and headed for the exit.

"We're headed for Southern California," Joe said as they cleared the gate. "Looks like this is going to be a grand tour around the country. C'mon out."

Joe stopped at a terminal near Los Angeles where he dropped the trailer he was hauling and picked up another trailer. Then he and Jesse headed north toward Sacramento. Joe left the freeway system for a few hours so that Jesse could see the beaches and the Pacific Ocean. She marveled at the surfboarders skimming through the waves and at the expanse of the ocean. She carefully traced their route on her US map and in her road atlas.

Joe also turned off the interstate when they got to Oregon, so that Jesse could see the Oregon coast. The craggy, boulder-strewn coast was much different from the sandy, seaweed strewn California coast. Jesse added a few more pictures to her collection. Joe spent much of the time commenting on the scenery they were passing. Joe suggested that Jesse put her window down so that she could feel the change in temperature and humidity as they traveled.

Frequently, Joe would pull into a truck stop to refuel the truck. His travel was orchestrated by the company so that he would be at a terminal complex after every twelve hours on the road. He was required to stop there for eight hours rest. When he took over the sleeper, Jesse curled up in the front seat. Joe warned her that terminals were often dangerous places and that she should never leave the truck when they were parked.

From Seattle, Joe was dispatched to the Denver area. He decided to get there by way of Salt Lake City and the Utah Salt Flats. He remembered fondly the quick dip that he and Mary had taken in the Great Salt Lake so many years ago. He didn't think it wise to offer the same chance to Jesse. Then came the Rocky Mountains. These elicited cries of wonder from Jesse. She was especially impressed by the amount of time it took them to get up into the mountains after she first sighted them. Slowly, Jesse was beginning to grasp the vastness of the United States.

After Denver, it was off to Omaha and the Great Plains. Jesse thought that they were boring.

It was just more of the same all day long. Then things got different in a hurry. Joe was dispatched to Madison, Wisconsin, where Jesse was able to try out some delicious cheeses. From there Joe drove south along Lake Michigan and through Chicago to New Hope, a little berg on the Pennsylvania – New Jersey border. Here he was able to show Jesse a little of what historic America was like.

From Pennsylvania, Joe headed south to Richmond, Virginia, by way of New York City, Washington, DC, and Arlington. Jesse was amazed by the enormity of New York and the majesty of Washington. But the site of the Arlington Cemetery, silenced her. Jesse had never shown true emotion, having the most even personality that either Joe or Mary had ever seen. But it took Jesse several hours to recover from seeing the vast number of graves and realizing that these were only a small number of those killed in wars.

Joe drove down the Atlantic coast to Jacksonville. Jesse was able to compare the Pacific and Atlantic coasts. Again the vastness of the ocean was a marvel to Jesse. From Jacksonville, Joe drove west along the Florida Gulf Coast for a little way then he turned up into the Appalachian Mountains and headed to Little Rock. Jesse was able to compare the Rockies and the Appalachians, but she was completely unaware that she had actually returned to her birthplace.

The layover at the Little Rock terminal was longer than usual. Instead of just dropping off the trailer, Joe had to wait while it was partially unloaded. He was now on his way home. There were no large loads headed toward Tucson. Joe's last stop was in San Antonio where he dropped off the last trailer and headed back towards Tucson, naked. Jesse was able to see the desert of central Texas and the gullies and arroyos of west Texas.

As they traveled toward Tucson, Joe had the chance to query Jesse about her experience. She now had a much better grasp of the size of the United States and of the various land formations and climates that comprised it. It would still take some time with her big atlas and her globe to work it all out, but at least she had the necessary information to make a good stab at it.

Jesse was also astounded by the crush of the large cities. So many people were crowded into such a small space. From Jesse's viewpoint there was a lot of very good land going to waste. Why would the people put up with such crowding? Joe did not have an answer to that question. More and more Jesse found herself contemplating questions and problems that had no solutions.

Even though Joe had no trailer, he had to stop by the Tucson terminal to turn in his logbook. Despite his several deviations from the most expeditious routes, Joe had managed to make all his deliveries on time. It was just that the sleep time Joe had recorded in his log was actually spent in large part driving.

Joe pulled into his yard at nine PM right on schedule.

Chapter 13

Mary Isn't Feeling Well

When Joe and Jesse pulled up at the house, all was dark: no outside lights and no light showing from any of the visible inside rooms. Joe stopped the truck with the door opposite the gate to the back yard.

"Okay, Jesse," he said as he shut off the engine. "Gather up your stuff, and any leftover food, but stay here in the truck until I tell you to get out."

Joe didn't want to sound worried, but this was definitely not the reception he was expecting. He knew he had called Mary from San Antonio and told her they would be home tonight.

He climbed down from the truck and opened the gate, swinging the sides of the gate apart to form an enclosed pathway from the truck to the yard. Joe went to the house and tried the back door. It was locked. He used his key to unlock the door and entered the laundry room.

Joe made his way carefully through the laundry room into the kitchen. There was still no visible light. He debated silently for a minute and then switched on the kitchen light. The kitchen was empty; nothing was out of place. But there was also no welcome-home dinner.

Joe moved on to the dining room. The light from the kitchen was sufficient to show that nothing was out of place here, either. He moved around the table and headed for the living room.

First, he checked the front door. It was closed and locked. Joe switched on the light.

Joe looked around the living room. There was something on the floor by the coffee table. Joe moved toward the couch. Then he saw Mary lying on the floor between the couch and the table. She was fully dressed; nothing seemed out of place. Joe quickly moved over to her, pushing the table out of the way.

Mary was breathing heavily, almost snoring. Joe tried to wake her, but she remained unresponsive. He was about ready to panic, but decided he needed more information before he called 9-1-1. Mary did not appear to be injured. There was no blood, no cuts or serious bruises. And she was definitely breathing. Since she did not seem to be in immediate distress, Joe looked around.

A bottle lying on the floor nearby attracted his attention. He picked it up and looked. It was an empty bottle of wine. Then he saw the wine glass, under the front edge of the couch. Was Mary drunk? Intoxicated maybe, but out cold? Besides, Mary didn't drink. Not since her experience with a glass of champagne at their marriage reception. After only one glass she had been so loopy she almost pulled both of them into the hotel pool. And, after the single bottle of beer at a barbecue, she had been trying to grill pancakes. Mary had an alcohol intolerance and she knew it. He couldn't get any answers until he could talk to Mary and that wasn't going to be possible until she sobered up.

Joe did not want Jesse to get antsy and walk in on this scene. There was only one thing to do. He picked Mary up and carried her into their bedroom. All he could do at the moment was to lay her on the bed and close the door. Then he went out to get Jesse.

Jesse, of course, had a million questions. Joe assured her that everything was all right. He suggested that Mary just wasn't feeling very good at the moment, but she would be better tomorrow. Jesse accepted that declaration at face value. She leaped down from the truck and helped Joe close and secure the gates.

Joe made a sandwich and Jesse finished off the last few bites of cheese. After they ate, Joe suggested a good night's sleep. Jesse agreed but before heading to her room she gathered up the rolls of film she had shot and gave them to Joe to be processed. Instead of just dropping off to sleep, Jesse spent some time reviewing the journal of her trip.

Joe managed to undress Mary and get her into bed. She did stir a bit during the process, but remained essentially asleep. Joe undressed, showered, set the alarm and crawled into bed beside Mary. He was immediately asleep.

The next morning, Jesse woke with the Sun as was her custom. She noted that Joe and Mary's bedroom door was closed as she made her way to the kitchen. She checked the refrigerator for breakfast. There was a half-full quart of milk – souring, but drinkable. No cheese, hard or cottage. One cup of yogurt. That, with a large glass of water, would be sufficient, for the moment.

Jesse was sitting at the kitchen table finishing off her breakfast when Mary wandered into the kitchen. She was wearing a simple blue flowered lounger. Her hair was a mess. "Good morning! I hope you are feeling better!" Jesse greeted her cheerily.

"Oh. You're home." Mary seemed a little woozy as she made her way to the counter to brew a cup of coffee. "Where's Joe?"

"I don't know. We got in last night." Jesse wasn't quite sure of Mary's condition, so she added, "Right on schedule." She glanced out the window. "The truck's gone."

Mary ignored her, leaning on the counter for support. So Jesse took advantage of the pause. "There doesn't seem to be anything in the house that I can eat. I think a trip to the store is in order."

"Maybe Joe went to the store", Mary offered as she gently sipped her cup of coffee.

"I've never known him to do the grocery shopping," Jesse observed. "That's always been your chore."

"Everything's my chore!" Mary complained. She walked slowly over to the table and sat down heavily, holding her head in her hands.

"Are you still ill? Do you have a headache?" Jesse was trying to sound caring, although that wasn't her true nature.

"Yeah, my head is splitting," was Mary's initial response. Then she quickly added, "But I'll be okay in a little bit. I just need some coffee."

Mary drained her cup and got up to pour a second cup. On her way back to the table she detoured to the pantry and looked inside. The she closed the pantry door and returned to the table.

Jesse had finished breakfast. She made one more attempt to get through to Mary, "Anything I can do to help?"

"No! I'll be okay!" Mary was almost pleading.

Jesse took the hint and headed out to the back yard. She would go over to the library later.

Joe returned to the house shortly after lunch and parked his truck in its usual place beside the house. Jesse had already left for the library. Mary was sitting in the living room watching her soap operas.

Joe didn't bother with any pleasantries. "Recovered from your binge?" he asked.

Mary looked up and bristled. "Where have you been?"

"I had to take the truck in for service. The appointment was marked on the calendar. Now, suppose you tell me what's going on. I come home from three weeks on the road and I find the house dark and you on the floor here in the living room passed out from an overdose of wine. I even called you and told you when I would be in."

Mary ignored him. She continued to stare at the television set.

Joe was getting frustrated. He walked over to the TV set and turned it off.

"Turn that back on!" Mary's attitude was becoming deliberately confrontational.

"Not until we have a chance to talk," Joe persisted calmly. "I want to know why you felt it was necessary to get soused on the day I was coming home. I want to know why there is so little food in the house. Especially food for Jesse. Are you no longer doing the household shopping?" Joe paused to catch a breath.

Mary sat back and crossed her arms across her chest. "There's no point in talking to you. It never does any good."

"When has it never done any good?" Joe was truly at a loss.

"I've talked 'til I'm blue in the face," Mary whined. "You never listen."

"What have you said?" Joe was getting confused. "What was I supposed to hear?"

"See? That's what I mean," Mary accused him. "You never pay any attention to me. Ever since you brought Jesse home it's always been you and Jesse. I've been completely left out. You even caused me to lose all my friends."

"You are the one who always wanted a baby," Joe said. Now he was truly confused. He wondered desperately what was really going on. "When I brought Jesse home with me, you agreed that we should keep her. I offered to leave her at a firehouse or hospital and you wouldn't hear of it. So we kept her and raised her. All I did was try to be a good father to her. As for your friends – that is your problem. I had nothing to do with it. I wasn't even here."

"That's right!" Mary yelled. "You weren't here. You're never here! When I said I wanted a baby, I meant a human baby; not that thing. What was I supposed to do with Jesse? I couldn't take her out with me, I didn't dare hire a sitter and I couldn't just leave her here alone. I was stuck here in the house with her for three weeks at a time. Then, when you do come home, you are always busy with chores and appointments and I'm still left alone."

"Okay, okay," Joe tried to calm her down. "You're upset. I get that. But, why the booze? You know you can't tolerate alcohol."

"When you and Jesse left," Mary said, becoming whiny again. "I thought I had a chance to get together with my friends again. I went to the library to play Scrabble on Tuesday. But there aren't any more Scrabble games. That evening I called Connie and found out that they are now plying Mahjong at the Tea Room, just down the street from the library.

"Next I tried to rejoin the Bridge group. They aren't playing party Bridge any more; they are playing 'duplicate'. They told me I had to fill out this crazy 'convention card'. It was a lot of mice type about conventions and bidding and leads. I couldn't make heads or tails of it, so I just put down standard American. It was a disaster! I got scolded for trying to rake in the cards when I won a trick. When my partner made a bid, the opponents asked me what she meant. I told them what I thought she meant and she frowned at me. When they asked her what my bid meant she just said she didn't know. At the end of the session they didn't have to ask me not to come back. I knew quite well that I didn't fit in anymore."

"Mary, I'm really sorry you ran into such problems," Joe tried his best to be supportive. "But, you've handled defeats like that before without getting drunk. Why the booze?"

"The next week I went to the Mahjong game at the Tea Room," Mary was almost in tears. "The Tea Room is a small café and wine bar. We met in the back room. I told them at the start that I didn't know anything about the game, so they paired me with another woman who could teach me as we played. That actually worked well, and I was having a good time. Then I was pressured into having a glass of wine with lunch. When I protested, my partner suggested a glass of *Riesling Spätlese*. I relented, just to go along with the group. I thought I would just sip a little. But when I tasted that light, smooth, fruity wine – I was hooked. It was absolutely delicious! I found that I could play much more easily, because I wasn't so worried about making a mistake.

"Then I found that I enjoyed the lonely afternoons at home more with a glass of wine. Apparently, I just got carried away yesterday." Mary rested her head in her hands. She was crying openly now.

Joe sat down on the couch next to Mary and put his arm around her. "Honey, I've done my best to include you. I even offered to take you with us on this last trip. We would have been together for three whole weeks. What more can I do?"

"I want you and me together," Mary pleaded, "like we used to be."

Joe completely misread that statement. He tried to pull Mary closer to him. She pushed away violently and refused to be budged.

"Get away from me!" She shouted.

Joe was hurt and confused. He did not know what else to do. "All right, be that way!" He responded. "I'm going out and do the grocery shopping!"

With that, Joe marched out the front door, got in the car and drove off. Mary continued sitting on the couch. She was still sobbing. No one noticed that Jesse had returned from the library early and had been sitting in the kitchen listening to most of the discussion.

Joe returned in two hours, somewhat calmer and with two large bags of groceries. The living room was empty as he passed through on his way to the kitchen. The kitchen was also empty, so Joe put the bags down and proceeded to put the groceries away. He stored the empty bags in the laundry room and then headed to the bedroom. Mary was nowhere to be found. Joe glanced into the back yard and saw Jesse sitting in her swing, with a book in her lap, slowly swinging back and forth.

Joe opened the window and called out, "Do you know where Mary is?"

"No," Jesse lied evenly. "She wasn't here when I got back from the library."

Mary did not return to the house until some time after supper. When Joe took his life in his hands and asked her where she had been, Mary simply answered, "Out!" She went back to their bedroom and closed the door. When Joe later headed to bed, he found the bedroom door locked.

Chapter 14

This Isn't Going to Work Forever

Joe was a tall man and rather lanky. He spent a most uncomfortable night on the living room couch. As a result, he did not get much sleep. He was sitting in the kitchen in jeans and a t-shirt nursing a cup of black coffee when Jesse got up and wandered in for breakfast.

Jesse glanced at the clock on the wall. It was already after nine. Mary was nowhere to be seen. "Isn't Mary up?" she asked.

"Not yet!" Joe continued staring intently at his coffee cup.

"I don't understand what is happening", Jesse confessed. "You and Mary have never acted this way before. What is going on?"

"You aren't the only one who doesn't understand, honey," Joe responded morosely. "I've never seen Mary act like this, either, and I don't know what is bothering her."

"Is she ill?" Jesse asked as she filled a glass with milk.

"That's hard to say," Joe hedged, " but I really don't think a doctor is going to do her any good."

Both Joe and Jesse looked up as they heard Mary coming through the living room. Mary was wearing a nice dress, jewelry and had make-up on. She acted as though nothing at all had happened. But, her voice was chilly when she announced that she was going out. Then she turned and marched out the front door without another comment. Joe and Jesse just looked at each other.

After Mary's departure Joe and Jesse went about their usual activities. Joe tended to chores. Jesse put on her wig and her clothes and headed back to the library. By now Jesse had an established routine. She would dress and start for the Library about ten in the morning. She would spend about four hours there either studying or just reading for pleasure and then head home. The librarian recognized her and willingly helped Jesse out whenever she had a problem she couldn't resolve.

Today, when Jesse got to the library she noticed Mary's car parked on the street at the side of the building. Jesse wondered what Mary could be doing at the library and why she hadn't offered a ride. When Jesse went into the library, she looked all over for Mary, but Mary was nowhere to be found.

When Jesse got back home that afternoon, Mary's car was parked in the driveway and Joe's truck was missing. Jesse went quietly into the back yard. It looked like Joe and Mary were still having problems. Which was indeed the case.

When Mary had returned home, Joe was sitting in the den going over the mail and paying bills. As Mary passed by the door, he called out to her, "Have a nice day?" She paused for a moment and looked at him. Joe held up the empty job jar, "Got all the chores done. Maybe we can spend some time together, now."

Mary stood still for a few more seconds. Then she just said, "I'm tired. I'm going to take a nap." She went on to their bedroom and closed the door behind her. Joe almost jumped up and followed her – almost. But at the moment he was looking at some strange charges on their credit card that he wanted to track down.

After waiting a few hours for Mary to reappear and prepare supper, Joe went to the bedroom door and knocked lightly. There was no response from within and the door was locked. Joe knocked more loudly and called out Mary's name. Still there was no response. Joe walked very deliberately out into the front yard and peered in through the window. The blinds had been drawn to block out the setting sun.

Joe was beginning to feel disgusted at Mary's behavior. He went back into the house, stopped by the den to fish a paper clip out of a desk drawer and returned to bedroom door. He knocked once more, saying, "Mary if you aren't going to let me in, I'm coming in anyway." There was no sound from the other side of the door. Joe used the paper clip to unlock the door and opened it.

Mary was lying on the bed in a dressing gown. There was a wine bottle on the bedside table and an empty glass was on the floor beside the bed. Mary was snoring heavily, but steadily. "Well", Joe thought, "tonight she's going to be in for a shock."

Joe fixed supper for Jesse and himself – again. After supper was over and the dishes cleaned up, Joe told Jesse that she was on her own. He was going to be occupied for the rest of the evening. He returned to the bedroom and closed the door behind him.

The yelling from behind that closed door woke Jesse from a sound sleep. She looked at her clock to learn that it was barely past midnight. Jesse could not make out what was being said, but the tone alone indicated that the fight was serious. After listening for a few minutes, Jesse gave up and headed for the roof. The night was clear and warm. There were a few lightning strikes visible up in the mountains. The yelling from inside the house was diminished. Still, Jesse had trouble getting back to sleep. She couldn't help but wonder at what was going on and how it would all come to affect her. She was also fighting a slight, but persistent headache.

The argument did not go well for either Joe or Mary. Joe could not get through to Mary that he was concerned about her – that her new drinking binge was not good for either of them. For her part, Mary denied being drunk, despite the nearly empty wine bottle. She also refused to discuss anything. She simply repeated that Joe did not understand her, did not care for her any more. The fact that he had been lying beside her when she woke up did not matter. She was, however, right about one thing: Joe did not understand why she was doing this.

The argument lasted for several hours with neither side gaining any advantage. Joe finally fired a fatal shot. "I'm not giving up," he stated flatly. "You say I don't care about you – well, I do care for you; I love you! I'm going to stick to you like glue. I'll go where you go, I'll do what you do. You're not going to lose me for a minute. If all you want to do is sit around and get drunk, then I'm going to sit around and get drunk with you."

At one point Mary jumped up, stormed out of the bedroom and staggered over to the living room couch. Joe followed her. When she laid down on the couch, Joe laid down on the floor in front of the couch. He figured that even if he eventually fell asleep, Mary couldn't leave the couch without waking him.

Mary only hesitated on the couch, then she was up and moving again. She went out to the kitchen and grabbed the car keys off the counter. Joe beat her to the door and blocked it. "You're in no condition to get behind the wheel of a car. If you really want to go somewhere, I'll be happy to drive you." Mary tried to push past Joe, but she could not match his size or strength. Finally she just crumpled into his arms sobbing.

For a few minutes, Joe just held Mary and let her cry. Then he gently guided her over to the couch where the two of them could sit down together. That is where Jesse found them when she came in for breakfast.

The argument had not been resolved, but it had been reduced to a more moderate level. Joe and Mary spent most of the day talking to each other. When talking wasn't working, Joe would take Mary in his arms and hold her until she would agree to talk again.

At the end of one of these hugs, Joe looked over at Mary and said, "You know, this can't last forever. I've got to go back on the road tomorrow. Are you going to be okay?" Mary nodded solemnly.

Chapter 15

Alone With The Demon

Jesse did not know what to expect when Joe went back on the road. But she had no reason to fear Mary. If Mary wanted to drink herself into oblivion, that was her business as far as Jesse was concerned. Jesse was not worried – neither did she foresee what was coming.

The afternoon of Joe's departure, Jesse made it a point to join Mary on the couch to watch soap operas. All went well. Mary did not pour herself any wine. The two had dinner together that evening. When the dishes were done, Jesse suggested laying out a jigsaw puzzle on the dining room table. Mary just said that she was going to bed.

After Jesse had been asleep for awhile, something awakened her. She lay quietly, wondering whether just to roll over and go back to sleep or if there was a reason to stay alert. There was a sound in the hallway. Jesse listened carefully. The sound was receding toward the living room. It had to be Mary wandering about, but it wasn't her usual gait. The steps were hesitant. There were several pauses. Eventually Jesse just rolled over and was soon asleep again.

Jesse awoke in the morning at her usual time and headed out to the kitchen for breakfast. As she passed through the living room she saw Mary lying in the middle of the floor, stark naked. Jesse hesitated just long enough to be sure Mary was only sleeping, then continued on to get some breakfast.

Mary was still sleeping soundly when Jesse went out to the back yard with a book. After a few attempts to send the swing over the top bar, Jesse decided to spend the morning on the roof. She was up there reading when she heard Mary's car leaving the driveway.

That afternoon it was raining lightly when Jesse went to the library. She saw Mary's car parked on the street. Jesse was about to duck into the library to dry off, but hesitated for a minute. There was no one on the street. She could see the sign for the Tea Room in the next block. Without knowing quite why, Jesse found herself walking down the street toward the Tea Room.

There was still no one out on the street as Jesse approached the café. There was a large window on either side of the door. Jesse edged up to the first window and peered inside. At first she couldn't see anything. Then she remembered her sunglasses and lifted them a bit. She could see Mary sitting alone near the back. There was a half-empty wine bottle on the table. Jesse turned and fled back to the library.

The rain stopped shortly after three and the sun came back in full force. Jesse looked for Mary's car when she started for home, but it was no longer parked by the library. Jesse just shrugged and headed home.

Jesse found Mary's car in the driveway and Mary on the living room couch. A bottle of wine and a glass were on the coffee table. Mary was considerably under the influence. "Can I do anything for you?" Jesse asked.

"No. Just leave me alone." Mary was slurring her words and had trouble even saying that much.

Jesse stored her books and went out to the back yard until supper time. By then Mary was sound asleep. So Jesse got something to eat and noted the depleted supply of edible food. She left a note for Mary. Not that she thought it would do much good.

Jesse turned in early, hoping for a good night's sleep. But she was once again awakened in the middle of the night by a shuffling sound in the hallway. She was about to just roll over and ignore it when she heard her bedroom door opening. Jesse didn't know whether to jump up and fight or to just pretend to be asleep. She compromised and slowly rolled over so she could see what was coming.

Although the room was quite dark, Jesse could make out Mary stumbling into her room. Mary got as far as the chair in the middle of the room and stopped, holding on to the chair for support. Then Mary squatted down and Jesse could hear the sound of running water. After a couple of minutes Mary struggled to stand up and stumbled out of Jesse's room, leaving the door open. Jesse waited a few minutes more, then she got up and quietly closed the door. The rug beside the chair was quite wet.

When Mary made her daily excursion, presumably to the Tea Room, Jesse wrapped up the rug from her room and took it out to the patio to wash. Using the garden hose and some dish soap from the kitchen, she managed to get the odor out of the rug. Then she hung it up on the swing set to dry. She made a mental note to get it down and back in her room before Mary returned.

Jesse added some items to the grocery list and taped it to the coffee machine where Mary would not be able to ignore it. She made it a point to stay out of Mary's way the rest of the day.

Jesse debated on spending the night up on the roof. She finally decided that Mary was a nuisance but otherwise presented no hazard. So she crawled into her bed for the night. But she couldn't get to sleep. She kept waiting for Mary to make her nighttime journey through the house. She still hadn't figured out what Mary did in the middle of the night, besides urinating in her room, that is.

Shortly after midnight, Jesse heard Mary shuffling out in the hall. She seemed to be talking to someone, but Jesse could not make out any response. Jesse lay quite still and waited for Mary's next trick. She didn't have to wait long.

Mary suddenly barged into Jesse's room. She was stumbling and obviously drunk. "I can't take this any more!" She was slurring her words and not making much sense. Jesse remained rigid, breathing slowly. Instead of stopping by the chair, Mary continued stumbling toward the bed. "You are the cause of all of my problems!" she blurted out. "Why can't you be more like a normal child?" When she reached the side of the bed, Mary began pummeling Jesse with her fists, still mumbling nonsense. The blows were a total surprise, but they were not severe.

Jesse did not know how to react, so she just lay there feigning sleep. The fact that no ordinary person would be able to sleep through a pounding was completely lost on Mary. Eventually, she tired of screaming at Jesse and beating on her and stumbled out of the room.

After Mary had gone, Jesse stretched and tested her arms and legs to make sure nothing was damaged. She did have a bit of a headache. That was unusual, but she just ascribed it to the pummeling. That was enough for Jesse, she spent the rest of the night up on the roof.

When morning came, Jesse stayed up on the roof. She had a lot to think about. Should she confront Mary about her nocturnal sojourns? Was Mary actually dangerous to her? So many questions and so few answers. In the end, Jesse opted for a direct approach. She decided to confront Mary before she left for the Tea Room.

Jesse was sitting in the living room as Mary headed toward the door on her way to the Tea Room. She stood up and blocked Mary's path. "We have to talk," she challenged Mary.

"I haven't got any time now, I'm late for Mahjong." Mary tried to push on by but Jesse didn't budge. "There is no Mahjong," Jesse answered. "There never has been. It was just an excuse to go to the Tea Room and get drunk."

"How dare you talk to me like that!" Mary was fuming.

"I dare since you started using my room for a toilet and beating on me as I slept." Jesse was adamant. "And since you decided to start starving me by not buying anything I can eat."

"I was just on my way to market. As for using your room for a toilet or beating you – that's totally absurd!" Given an opening, Mary was becoming self-righteous.

"I'll believe that when I see you coming home sober with the groceries." Jesse challenged Mary.

"You ungrateful little wretch! Who rescued from the desert? Who gave you everything you have: a playground, a comfortable home, all the books you wanted?"

"I know what I know," Jesse persisted. "And when Joe comes home, he will know it, too."

"You'll tell Joe nothing! Do you hear me? You are grounded. You will not leave this house again!" Mary was shouting. "Now, get out of my way!" She pushed by Jesse and out the door.

"That didn't go well," Jesse thought to herself as she went into the kitchen for breakfast. She found the last little bit of milk and cheese in the refrigerator. And then searched for anything else edible. There was nothing that didn't contain plant matter. When she went to toss the milk carton in the garbage she found something else on top – the wadded up grocery list.

Jesse presumed that 'house' included the back yard, so she grabbed a book and went out to the pool to await Mary's return

Mary returned at mid afternoon, as usual. She was already quite drunk. She was carrying a bag with her, but had brought no groceries. Jesse met her as she entered the living room. "And where are the groceries you went after?" Jesse asked.

"Get out of my way!" Mary slurred. She pushed past Jesse and took her bag to the kitchen and stowed the contents, several bottles, in the pantry.

After Mary had left the kitchen, Jesse examined the bottles that Mary had brought home. There were three bottles of wine and two smaller bottles of vodka. Jesse didn't know what vodka was, but she correctly perceived that it was probably intoxicating.

Now Jesse had a truly pressing problem – food. There was nothing in the house that she could eat. Jesse had looked carefully in the pantry. There was plenty of food, but it all contained vegetable matter of some sort. And Jesse's body automatically rejected vegetable matter. The refrigerator was likewise bereft of anything edible. And there weren't any calories in water.

Jesse thought briefly of going to the market, but she did not know where the markets were – and she didn't have any money. Well, one day without food wouldn't kill her. She would try again tomorrow.

Chapter 16

I'm Not Lying

The next day Jesse again met Mary as she was leaving the house. This time she demanded that Mary bring home something that she could eat. Again, Mary promised that she would do so. Again, Mary came home drunk and without the necessary food.

Jesse had been planning for just this eventuality. She knew she had to have food to survive and she knew where she could find it. She also knew that she was crossing the line of acceptable behavior. But she was going to teach Mary a lesson, even if it meant personal disaster.

Sometimes, when she was out on the roof at night, Jesse had seen a cat prowling around the neighborhood. Tonight, Jesse waited and watched for that cat. Shortly after midnight She saw the cat out on the prowl. She waited patiently until the cat approached the backyard fence.

Jesse leaped off the roof onto the fence and ran full speed along the top of the fence. The cat did not have time to sense her approach. Jesse leaped off the fence and speared the cat with the plates on the bottom of her feet. With the cat pinned to the ground, Jesse had no trouble at all snapping its neck. Then she picked up the cat and leaped back to the top of the fence and into the back yard.

The cat was obviously feral and quite scrawny, but it was food. Jesse skinned the cat carefully, retaining as much of the meat as possible. She ate ravenously without bothering to cook the meat. She was putting her sharp teeth to good use.

Once she had finished off all of the meat, Jesse put the entrails back into the carcass and took it into the house. Jesse moved as quietly as possible and made her way back to Mary's bedroom. She slowly opened the door and peeked inside.

Mary was asleep on her bed, snoring heavily. Jesse snuck into the room and placed the cat's carcass on the floor next to the bed. It was in a spot where Mary would have to step on it as she arose from the bed. Jesse attached a clearly worded not to the carcass stating her need for food. Then she crept out of the room and silently closed the door. Just to be on the safe side, Jesse spent the rest of the night up on the roof, safely out of Mary's grasp.

The next morning the shriek was heard all over the neighborhood. As Jesse had planned, Mary stepped on the cat carcass with her bare feet as she got out of bed. When she did so, the entrails were squeezed out, all over her feet.

Mary tore into Jesse's room and began pounding on the shape in the bed. It was only after a full minute's pounding that Mary realized she was hitting a pillow. She turned and rushed out of the room into the hall. There, she was stopped in her tracks by Jesse, leaning nonchalantly against the wall at the end of the hall.

"I told you that I was out of food." Jesse said defiantly. "I really suggest that you go to the store today. Otherwise, I may be forced to eat

113

something else." Jesse was staring directly at Mary when she uttered those last few words.

Mary started to move toward Jesse with murder in her eye, but Jesse didn't budge and didn't waver in her stare. Before she had taken two steps, the message sank in. Mary stopped in her tracks, turned around and returned to her room, entering gingerly.

Jesse was in the kitchen nursing a glass of water when Mary entered. She was dressed casually in a pair of Capri's. "Jesse, I am so sorry!" Mary began. "I didn't know what I was doing! I am really going shopping this morning. I am not lying to you. I will try to get enough food to last you until Joe gets home."

Jesse looked up slowly. Mary sounded quite contrite but she had lied before.... "I think I have heard that before," she said quietly and evenly. "Are you sure you don't want a drink before you leave?" Jesse was almost sorry that she said that, almost.

"Jesse," Mary said, "I can't promise you that I won't drink again. But at least I am going to try to reduce the amount. I know it's going to take a lot to regain your trust. Will you give me a chance?"

"All I can say," Jesse responded evenly, "is that there will be no more dead cats – as long as the food holds out."

With that, Mary turned and left the house. About two hours later she returned with several bags of groceries. Jesse even came in and helped her put the food away. Jesse saw no additional bottles of wine or vodka.

Jesse was always ready to be agreeable, so when the groceries had been put away, she asked, "Can we do something together?"

"Thank you for the offer," Mary said, "but I've got a lot of thinking to do and I'm going to have to do it alone. Oh, by the way – you are no longer grounded. But do be careful. And no more dead cats!"

The day passed without further incident. Jesse returned to her usual schedule of visiting the library. Mary was cordial but distant all day. Mary and Jesse spent the night in their respective rooms. Both were doing a lot of thinking.

The next morning Mary beat Jesse to the kitchen for breakfast. She was scrambling some eggs as Jesse walked in. "I made enough for two. Want some?"

"Sure," Jesse answered. She went to the fridge and got some shredded cheese to add to her portion of egg. "What's on your agenda today?" Jesse asked between mouthfuls.

"I think I'm actually going to try to track down that Scrabble club", Mary said.

As Jesse left for the library, she saw Mary sitting on the couch with her address book making telephone calls.

When Jesse returned, Mary was still sitting on the couch, but now she appeared quite drunk. Her address book was lying on the floor half way across the room. Apparently her attempts to locate the Scrabble club, or to wangle an invitation to return to it, had not been successful. Jesse almost grimaced with the thought that things were already 'back to normal'.

That evening the phone rang. Mary was sitting next to it sound asleep. Despite its constant ringing, Mary slept on. Jesse heard the phone, but she had been strictly warned never to answer it – no matter what. Jesse was almost sure that it Joe who was calling. This time, Jesse ignored what she had been told.

She picked up the handset and ventured a quiet, "Hello?"

Joe was indeed on the other end of the line, but he could not make out the sound that he heard. "Hello! Who is this?" Then the situation became clear. "Is this Jesse?"

Jesse did her best. "Joe, this is Jesse. Can you hear me?" Jesse's voice, understandable to the human ear, was being garbled by the inner workings of the telephone system.

Joe, hearing nothing intelligible, thought quickly. "Jesse, if this is you and you can hear me, tap the handset once." The response was a single tap. "Okay, Jesse one tap for 'yes', two taps for 'no', three for 'I don't know'. Are you okay?" Tap.

Joe breathed easier. "Is Mary there?" Tap. "Is she drunk?" Tap.

"Okay, Jesse, when Mary sobers up, please tell her that I will not be home Friday. I have a longer drive back to Tucson than usual and will be in Saturday night instead. Do you understand?" Tap. "Love you, Jesse. Take care!"

Jesse carefully put the phone back in the cradle. Ordinarily, a day's delay in Joe returning would not be a big deal. But with Mary in her current condition, anything might happen in that short interval.

Chapter 17

Is There a Way Out?

The night passed calmly. Once or twice Jesse heard Mary stumbling up and down the hall, but she never entered Jesse's room. Jesse also heard her speaking out loud once. Jesse could not make out what was being said. It sounded like Mary was arguing with someone.

When Mary came out for her breakfast coffee, Jesse delivered the message from Joe. "Why did you answer the phone?" Mary demanded. "Haven't I told you never to answer the phone? Why didn't you call me?"

"Yes, you told me, but you were sitting next to the phone and were ignoring it. You were in no condition to answer it. I thought it might be Joe with something important."

"That doesn't matter! Why can't I depend on you to do what you are told?"

Jesse took another sip of milk and ignored Mary's last question. Jesse attempted to end the discussion with, "Message received; message delivered." She got up, rinsed out her glass and headed out to the back yard. Mary just sat at the table with her head in her hands.

Jesse was again suffering from a minor headache. Jesse had recently been getting little aches and pains quite frequently. Sometimes they were in her head, sometimes in her lower abdomen. They never were severe and they didn't last very long. They were just a nuisance. Jesse did not know what was causing them, but she was pretty sure it wasn't just this business with Mary.

As he had predicted, Joe pulled his truck up the side of the house on Saturday evening. When he acme into the house he found Jesse in the kitchen putting the finishing touches on a meal of salad, penne and sausage. Joe took one whiff of the delightful aroma, then he looked around. "Where's Mary?" he asked.

"She's not feeling well," Jesse answered. "I cooked this up myself. I hope you like it. Why don't you get washed up?"

After a second helping, Joe congratulated Jesse on another remarkable achievement and helped her clean up the dishes and put away the leftovers. He was quite pensive. "How has Mary been behaving?" he asked.

"Just the same", Jesse answered. "She goes out in the morning and drinks somewhere, probably the Tea Room. Then she comes home and finishes the job. By bedtime she has usually passed out."

"Has she been bothering you much?" Joe sounded honestly worried.

"I haven't given her the chance," Jesse replied. "I've been avoiding her."

"I was thinking about this while I was on the road," Joe said flatly. "It's got to stop. I think I have a plan. It's drastic and a last resort, but I don't think we have a choice if we are going to save Mary from herself. You don't have to have anything to do with it, but I could sure use your help."

"What are we going to do?" Jesse wasn't too sure she wanted to get involved, but she could at least listen to the details.

"While Mary is sleeping off her latest drunk, we are going to go through this house from top to bottom, every cupboard and crevice and find all her bottles. Whatever we find, we'll bring into the kitchen."

The two started by going through the kitchen: the pantry, the cupboards, the refrigerator, the stove, everything. They followed this up with the dining room cabinets, the living room, the foyer. Then Joe went through his office while Jesse searched her room and the hall bathroom. As an afterthought, Jesse went out to search the laundry room while Joe investigated Mary's car.

So far they had a total of six full wine bottles, two partial bottles, 3 pints of vodka, two pints of gin and one of bourbon. Joe left Jesse to empty out all the bottles into the sink and wash it down the drain. He went to his bedroom where he found Mary sound asleep. He moved carefully about the room searching for more bottles. He came away with two partial bottles of wine and one of vodka. These he added to the stash in the kitchen.

When all of the bottles had been emptied and lined up on the counter by the sink, Joe and Jesse called it a night. They planned to be up and back in the kitchen by first light.

And so, when Mary wandered into the kitchen the next morning and saw the bottles lined up on the counter she was stunned. She just stood in the doorway staring.

"Come on in and sit down," Joe suggested rather firmly. Mary started to protest, then simply did as she was told.

"Mary, your binge drinking has got to stop. It's tearing this family apart. I suppose I could just divorce you, but I do love you and we're going to give this one more try. This is your last way out.

"I have stopped your charge card and moved our money to another bank under my name. I also cleaned out your purse and the petty cash fund. You will not be leaving the house to buy liquor. I have your car keys and the car has been disabled; it will not run. You are restricted to this house. If you have to leave either Jesse or I will accompany you. You can start sessions at Alcoholics Anonymous, see a private therapist, go to a rehab center or go to a mental hospital. Your choice. But it is no longer going to be business as usual. Do you understand?"

"You're crazy!" was Mary's enlightened response.

"No, not crazy," Joe said evenly. "I am sad. I am disappointed in you. And I still want this marriage to work."

"And just what are you going to do when you have to go back on the road?" Mary challenged him. "Or do you plan on quitting your job?"

"That's the icing on the cake, my dear," Joe said just a bit too sweetly. "If you haven't at least started to straighten out, preferably in a rehab center by the end of the week, I have a special treat for you. I will hog tie you, put on a blindfold and gag and throw you in the back of my truck. Somewhere on one of my runs I will simply leave you beside the road. You will have no clothes, no money and no identification. You can either find a way to get back home or just go get drunk. By then I probably won't care which."

"You wouldn't dare!" Mary was furious.

"Don't test me! Joe threw right back at her. "From now on, Jesse and I will have you under constant surveillance. Let me know what you decide." Joe waited a few seconds for his ultimatum to sink in. Then he simply asked, "Coffee?"

Mary just sat there. She was obviously stunned at the turn of events. She got up and headed back to the bedroom. On the way she met Jesse coming toward the kitchen with two more bottles. "Just fished these out from under your mattress," she said in passing. "I bet your bed will feel much more comfortable now."

The next day, Mary had made her decision. She would go to rehab. Joe was battling sensations of happiness and sorrow. Jesse reserved judgment. Mary packed a small suitcase and Joe drove her down to the rehab center and signed her in. Her input paperwork stipulated that she would be at the center for twelve weeks. She would have to earn any days outside by following the rules and participating in the therapy sessions. The contract also stipulated that she could only leave the center when Joe was available to chaperone her.

When Joe retuned, it was obvious to Jesse that he had been crying. "Now we have another problem," he said to Jesse. "What am I going to do with you?"

"I'll be fine here by myself," Jesse insisted. She was just getting an inkling of what Joe had in mind. One trip around the country had been fun and educational. Any more such trips would be boring.

"What about food?" Joe asked. "You can't use the telephone and you know nothing about shopping or money or credit cards. Besides, it still isn't safe for you to venture out in public."

Jesse thought for a minute, then asked, "Can't you buy enough food to last me until you get back from your tour?"

"I suppose so," Joe replied. "And I guess someone ought to be here if Mary should suddenly turn up."

"She wouldn't!" Jesse exclaimed; "Would she?"

"I wouldn't put anything passed Mary," Joe mused, "but it isn't probable. They will keep pretty close control over her at the rehab center."

Chapter 18

Decision Time

When Joe departed on his next road trip, Jesse found herself really alone in the house. For the first time in her life she was on her own. There was no one around to help her out when she got into trouble. Jesse wandered around the house, just going from room to room. It felt strange.

Jesse thought about going to the library to break the monotony. Originally, the library had been a source of information. In the last few months it had become a refuge from a drunken mother. Now, what use would it be? Try as she might, Jesse could not find an answer to that question. "Besides," she thought, "if she were to leave the house now, there would be no one around to rescue her if she got into trouble."

At first Jesse divided her time among reading, watching TV and exercising out in the back yard. Nothing was really interesting. She was still recovering and decompressing from the time she had spent with Mary. The pressure was off now. There was no immediate threat. Still, Jesse felt uneasy. She had not yet learned the term for what she was going through. She was also still having periodic bouts of pain.

There was nothing to prevent Jesse from getting a good night's sleep in her own bed – or in any other bed in the house – but Jesse still spent every clear night up on the roof. She felt most comfortable just staring up at the stars.

One night, as she lay on the roof, a stray thought wafted through her mind. Mary had once said that Jesse was the cause of all her problems. That had bothered Jesse when she said it and it still bothered her. As she lay there under the stars, Jesse pondered that.

Jesse had always tried to be kind to Mary and Joe. She obeyed them as well as she understood. She hadn't even started collecting Mary's bottles until Joe had suggested it – and long after Mary had made that statement. How could she have been the cause of Mary's problems? Mary had never explained that remark. Jesse had been too ashamed to ever ask her to. Now the thought kept rattling around her mind, preventing her from getting any sleep. It had to be dealt with, despite the headache that was starting again.

Jesse kept reliving the past, searching for something she had said or done which could have prompted Mary's comment. She couldn't remember anything. Maybe, she thought, it was the trip she took with Joe. Was Mary jealous? But Mary had been invited to go along. "Mary must have known," Jesse thought, "that there was no way that Joe could have had any romantic interest in me." Still, that would explain the comment. No, it was not possible, and certainly not feasible. It had to be something else.

Eventually, Jesse did fall asleep. But the question did not leave her. Every day the question would pop up, over and over again. No matter how hard Jesse tried, she could not find an answer. Then one day, as she turned on her favorite TV show, she discovered that it had been preempted by a political debate. Jesse was fuming, when she saw a notice on the bottom of the screen that said her show was on an alternate channel. It was a simple thing to switch channels, far better than just getting mad.

As Jesse was sitting on the couch watching her program, it suddenly came to her. If you have a problem bringing in your program, change channels. That somehow made perfect sense. If Jesse was having trouble figuring out what she had done to cause Mary a problem, maybe she should look elsewhere.

That one thought broke the logjam. If it wasn't something that Jesse had said or done that was the problem, what else could it have been? Mary had said, "You are the cause of all my problems." Maybe, Jesse should just take the statement at face value. She, herself, was the cause of the problems. It wasn't something she had done, it was simply the fact the Jesse existed!

Jesse tried to remember what she had been told of her origin. Joe had found her as a baby lying on the side of the road. He had brought her home with him and he and Mary had decided to adopt her. She had once asked Joe why he and Mary didn't have children. He answered that he couldn't provide any viable sperm. It took Jesse a few trips to the library to decipher that comment.

So, Mary had wanted children, but couldn't have any from Joe. Joe wanted Mary to have children and picked Jesse up off the side of the road. Why was that a problem?

Jesse reran the script. She was the problem. So, then baby is good; Jesse is bad. Jesse knew she was different. She had some time ago figured out that she was not a human. After all, she had been warned not to go out of the house lest someone see her and realize she wasn't human. She had been told many times that if the authorities got their hands on her she would end up in a laboratory somewhere and never again see the light of day.

Jesse was beginning to figure it all out. She was bad – and the cause of Mary's problems – because she wasn't human. Mary wanted to show off her new baby, but she couldn't show off Jesse. That was it! She was the cause of Mary's problems because Mary couldn't be seen with her. Nor could Mary leave the baby at home alone, nor could she safely get a nanny for her.

It all suddenly became clear to Jesse. She couldn't imagine the pressure and stress Mary was operating under. No wonder she turned to sedatives! She just picked the wrong kind of sedative. She was never really mad at Jesse; she was under the affect of the alcohol she was using to make her own pain and discomfort bearable. This realization gave Jesse a much different concept of Mary. It did not detract from Mary's need for treatment. But it did explain a lot.

Jesse had spent some time learning about rehab. It was supposed to keep people from drinking so that they could face their problems realistically and resolve them. If Jesse were the cause of Mary's drinking binges, how could she ever resolve the problem without discussing Jesse with her counselors? Mary would have to admit that she had an alien child. If Mary did that, Jesse would be in dire trouble. If Mary didn't tell the counselor about Jesse, she could never get to the bottom of her drinking problem.

That gave Jesse a new problem to ponder. Was there something that she could do, or should do, to improve the situation? If the mere presence of Jesse was causing Mary such severe problems, then Mary could never get truly well while Jesse was in the house. The obvious solution was for Jesse to leave the house. But where would she go? How would she survive? What about the authorities?

Jesse was not worried. There was no need for an immediate decision. Maybe she should wait until Joe returned and talk everything over with him. He might know of someplace in the country where she would be safe. She decided that she would take her time and think about it.

Chapter 19

Escape!

Now that she had a basic plan for her future, Jesse was counting the days until Joe would return from his road trip. She very much wanted to ask his advice about her plan. She was not prepared for what happened next.

Jesse was sitting in the living room one morning rereading one of her favorite novels when she heard a car drive up to the curb in front of the house. Jesse peeked out of the front window. She saw a taxi, from which emerged ... Mary! There was no way Mary could have legitimately left the rehab center in only two weeks. But there she was, arguing with the taxi driver and heading toward the house.

Jesse knew that all the doors were locked, but she couldn't be certain that Mary didn't have a key. Jesse sprinted to her room and out the window. She teetered perilously on the outside window ledge while she closed the window tightly. Then she leaped to the roof of the shed and to the roof of the house.

Jesse crept to the front of the house and listened carefully at a drain port. The taxi driver wanted to be paid. Mary said that she would pay him as soon as she got some money from inside the house. The driver was torn between waiting in his cab and following Mary to the house. Finally, he chose the latter option.

Mary got to the front door and searched for the key that had been hidden in the sand beside the stoop. She came up empty. Joe had removed all the hidden keys before he left. He cautioned Jesse to hide a key if she ever left the house and to retrieve it when she returned. But Jesse would be using the back door, not the front.

Mary was unhappy. The taxi driver was unhappy. It was also clear that Mary had been drinking. Her speech was slightly slurred. "There's got to be a key around here somewhere."

"Look, lady," the exasperated drive was saying, "all I want is my fare. Then you can look forever for all I care."

"I haven't any money," Mary slurred out. "I've got to get inside." With that Mary tried the door again, and still got nowhere.

"You got me to drive all the way out here and you knew you had no money to pay!?" the taxi driver was irate. "I'm calling the police!" With that he turned and headed back to his cab.

Mary made her way, not too steadily, to the back gate. That she also found tightly secured. She looked up at the top of the fence, probably with the idea of climbing over it Thinking batter of the idea, she headed back to the front of the house, trying windows as she went.

In the meantime, the taxi driver had used his radio to tell his dispatcher where he was and to summon the police to pick up a deadbeat. Before Mary could try all of the front windows, a police car arrived. The police officer conferred briefly with the driver and then walked up to the house where Mary was again searching for the key.

"Good afternoon, ma'am," the officer began. "Could you please show me some identification?"

"I'm afraid I don't have my purse,." Mary offered. "If I can get into the house, I will have money and ID."

"How do I know that this is your house?" the officer asked.

"Because I tell you it is!" Mary's speech was still slurred.

"I'm afraid that's not good enough," the officer stated. "Is there someone you can call who will vouch for you?"

"No, my husband drives trucks," Mary said rather curtly. "He's away right now."

"Well, now that puts me in a bad spot, The officer explained as calmly as he could. "You owe this driver over ten dollars, you're obviously trying to break into this house, which you can't prove you own, and from the smell of your breath you are on the way to a great hangover. Altogether that amounts to petty larceny, attempted B&E and public drunkenness. You're going to have to come with me."

When the police officer took Mary's arm to lead her back to the police car, she jerked her arm away and tried to slug the officer. In less than 10 seconds she was in handcuffs being escorted most un-gently to the back seat of the police car.

Jesse remained well concealed on the roof until the taxi and police car had left the area. She had no idea what course things might follow from this point. Mary could not have legitimately left the rehab center. Would she be returned there? Would they reject her as a patient and turn her loose? How long would it take to contact Joe and verify Mary's identity?

The roof was getting really hot in the noon-day sun. Jesse got up and sprinted to the back edge by the shed. Without breaking stride, she jumped to the roof of the shed and continued across it. At that point, it was a simple task to leap off the shed and into the pool in the back yard. The cool water was quite refreshing. Jesse lounged in the pool for awhile and continued her thoughts.

Mary was proving to be unreliable. How did she get alcohol in the rehab center? If she escaped from the rehab center first, how could she pay for the alcohol without any money? Or, Jesse was recalling some of the television programs she had watched, what did she have to do to get the alcohol?

It was obvious that Mary's need for alcohol was what was driving her at this point. That was not likely to change in the short term. Joe had his hands full. He would have no time, and little energy to deal with her and Mary. Jesse realized that taking herself out of the picture might not be the solution, but it would help.

If Jesse were to leave, it would have to be soon. She needed a plan and she would have to develop it without Joe's assistance. First, she needed a location. Where could she go? Where would she find her people? She didn't know. But she had a clue. Joe said he found her beside the road that led through the Indian reservation north of Tucson. That would do for a start.

Jesse got out her map collection and planned her route. She could go south to Valencia, then west until she could turn north around Tucson. Eventually, she wanted to get to highway 77, which would take her up toward the reservation.

132

Her primary objective was not a direct path, but one that would allow her to remain as invisible as possible.

When to go was another concern. This was the rainy season for Tucson. There were frequent thunderstorms. The rain didn't bother Jesse; it would help to hide her as she moved out of the Tucson area. There were storms predicted for the end of the week. That would be her target date.

Now, all Jesse had to do was wait – and hope that Mary would not show up again. But, just to be on the safe side, Jesse kept a close watch during the day and slept up on the roof at night.

The days passed so slowly that time just seemed to drag. Finally the weekend came. The sky was cloudy and rain was predicted for the evening commute. Jesse packed a small purse with some food. She debated about wearing clothing. She felt it would impede her movement and slow her down in the rain. But she couldn't really put on any speed while she was around Tucson. It would attract too much attention to see some small person zooming around in the rain. She decided to start out wearing clothing, especially through Tucson.

About eight PM the rain was coming down hard. Jesse put her wig on with a double dose of tape, just in case. She thought about putting on her facial makeup, but decided that the rain was heavy enough to just wash it off. And smeared was worse than none. She dressed in her tights and a shirt and put on shoes. As an afterthought, she put on the cap Joe had bought her during their trip together and pulled it down over her forehead. Carrying her purse of food, Jesse left the only home she had ever known, carefully locking the

door behind her, and started on her fateful journey
to find her people.

Epilogue

This has been a tale of fear and how it affected the various participants.

After Joe struck Lisa in the desert, he was afraid to report the incident. He feared the possible loss of his drivers license. How different our tale would have been had he simply chosen to report the incident to the reservation sheriff.

But Joe still had options. Unfortunately, he was afraid to leave the baby at a hospital or fire station because his truck might be identified.

Then Joe and Mary had to decide what to do with the baby once she had been taken to their house. They chose to keep her and raise her. Even when Mary learned the baby's true nature, she chose to keep her and protect her. Both Joe and Mary feared what the authorities might do to the baby.

But living with an alien, even one as agreeable as Jesse proved to be, can put severe strain on any relationship. Mary bore the brunt of that strain. It was up to her to keep the family together. And doing so it cost her dearly. Her daily routine was completely disrupted because she feared how her friends would react to the baby. She felt trapped in the house, because she feared the reaction of a babysitter. She lost her entire social support group, leaving her isolated and vulnerable.

Joe simply went back to driving. After all, 'Mary had always wanted a baby', and Jesse was a baby. He did not know how to handle the strain that was plaguing Mary. Besides, someone had to earn a living to support the family.

When the stress and strain became too great, Mary resorted to wine, the delicious elixir of the gods, to dull her mind and, for a few hours at least, allow her to ignore the pain she was feeling. Her intolerance to alcohol proved her undoing.

For her part, Jesse, was also experiencing the stress and strain of trying to remain unnoted as she moved about the human world. Then, at the end, there was the fear of Mary and what she might decide to do to her. When a child must, of necessity, fear a parent things have totally gotten out of hand.

Then there were Jesse's aches and pains. They were becoming more frequent and, at the end, included abdominal pains as well. There was no one to whom Jesse could talk to about them. And Jesse did not have a clue as to their cause or meaning. She could only suffer in silence. Eventually, continued suffering was no longer an option.

All of this, of course, is just human nature at work and was predictable from the beginning. What was not predictable was Mary's impact on Jesse. When she taught Jesse about arithmetic, and showed her that little table of numerical relationships, she gave Jesse the information she would need in the future to save the Elder people.

Our story does not end here. It will be continued in Volume 4 of The Elder Chronicles, 'The Legend of Red Hawk'

== 30 =

Also by Robyn Kelly:

The Elder Chronicles: The Lost World

The Elder Chronicles: Birth of a Savior

Watch for volume four of The Elder Chronicles: The Legend of Red Hawk

Coming Soon!

www.ingramcontent.com/pod-product-compliance
Lightning Source LLC
Chambersburg PA
CBHW030625130626
46552CB00002B/710